YA
L
Paperback Shelf
W9-BFJ-183
Mark Leonard
Psalms 19:1-2
DATE DUE

Let There Be Light

Mark Leonard

WestBow Press books may be ordered through booksellers or by contacting:

WestBow Press
A Division of Thomas Nelson & Zondervan
1663 Liberty Drive
Bloomington, IN 47403
www.westbowpress.com
1 (866) 928-1240

ISBN: 978-1-4908-7299-5 (sc)
ISBN: 978-1-4908-7300-8 (hc)
ISBN: 978-1-4908-7301-5 (e)

Library of Congress Control Number: 2015903960

Print information available on the last page.

WestBow Press rev. date: 05/18/2015

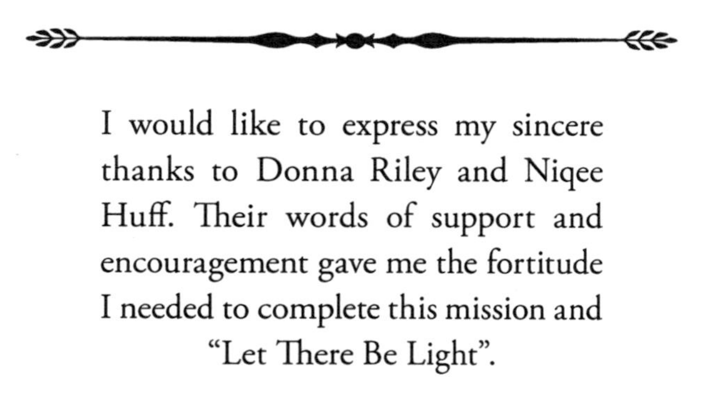

I would like to express my sincere thanks to Donna Riley and Niqee Huff. Their words of support and encouragement gave me the fortitude I needed to complete this mission and "Let There Be Light".

INTRODUCTION FROM THE AUTHOR

Our young people are being bombarded with the "fact" of evolution through our school systems and the media. Students feel they have no choice but to believe the evolutionary teachings that millions of years of gradual change are what shaped our planet into what it is today. These students feel there is no way the stories of Genesis or the possibilities of a young earth scenario could be true. And if you can't believe in the first few chapters of the Bible, why should you believe the rest of it?

Recently, science has uncovered facts showing this earth did not evolve gradually. Catastrophic events occurred changing the face of the planet. But we do not hear about these findings in main stream media or the classroom. If a discovery does not meet the evolutionary mold, it is thrown out as not being viable.

This book, in a fictional setting, reveals many of these discoveries showing catastrophic changes did occur. And these findings coincidentally concur with the events spelled out in the scripture.

Join Bill Abrams on an adventure of a lifetime. And maybe you too will discover, just as I did, that science does prove the Bible to be historically correct. I still remember the day when the proverbial "light bulb" came on for me, and I realized Genesis is true. And if Genesis is true – I would bet the rest of it is too.

CHAPTER ONE

The stainless steel elevator doors slid open revealing a pitch black room. Bill Abrams jumped from the elevator proclaiming, "Let there be light!" The motion detectors activated a series of florescent lights illuminating the underground laboratory.

Michael Hansen shook his head as he exited the elevator. "Let's get the equipment we came for and get on with this little excursion of yours before Mr. Hackman finds out what we are doing."

"Come on," Bill reasoned. "Here we are in Barrow, Alaska, doing an ice core study for the U.S. government, and what do we discover?" Without letting Michael respond, Bill exclaimed, "A camel! We have a chance to go down and look at this thing and you don't want to risk it? We could end up on the cover of Archeology Today with this find!"

"You know as well as I do, we were hired by the government to do a study on the global warming phenomenon and how the melting ice caps are going to affect our ocean levels," Michael rebutted. "Not how our polar ice caps seem to be sitting on a tropical haven of quick frozen plants and animals."

"I know," Bill responded, "but doesn't it seem odd how our ice cores have brought up so many things that do not belong in this area of the planet? And now, after hitting this ice cavern yesterday, we have a chance to see one of these specimens up close and personal."

"I still think Mr. Hackman is going to find out about this, and we will not receive the final installment of our compensation package. And you know what you would have to deal with then?" Michael paused while staring at Bill. "The wrath of Becky!"

"Okay," Bill said grabbing the last piece of equipment. "Then let's get going before anyone finds out."

In less than an hour, Bill had flown the two-person Piper Cub plane to the work site, landing a good distance from the hole that had been drilled the day before. They didn't want the vibrations to disturb what lay below. About 200 meters down, the core drill had struck an ice cavern, and then traveled another 100 meters of open air before hitting the ice again. Directly below that surface, they had brought up the remains of an animal. The DNA showed it was from a camel indigenous to northern Africa.

They lowered a camera through the hole and discovered the cavern traveled approximately 50 meters in all directions. The camera could also make out the faint shadow of an animal below the surface of the ice. Just before nightfall, they had attached the largest drill available digging a 24 inch hole into the cavern.

Now the time had come to lower one of them into the cavern. "Let's do rock, paper, scissors, to see who gets to go!" Bill suggested.

"We have already been over this," Michael explained. "I have had classes in rappelling while you have a better idea how to run a gas powered winch. Let's just do our jobs and get out of here."

Bill consented while putting his headset on. "You've got your ears on?"

"Check." Michael answered.

"Is the camera ready to go?" Bill inquired.

Michael held up the device indicating he had a fresh battery pack in his pocket.

"Now, get your oxygen flowing," Bill instructed. "We have no idea what the air quality is like in this cavern that's been sealed up for thousands of years. You've got 30 minutes on that tank and should be okay."

A small seat was attached to the cable. Michael hunched his shoulders as the winch lowered him down the tight shaft. The light on his yellow hard hat illuminated the side wall of the freshly drilled hole. The ice turned from a clear tone to a bluish hue the further down he went. This indicated more of the oxygen had been pressed out over the years from the weight of the ice.

"I'm just entering the cavern," Michael reported back to Bill. "Keep it slow and steady."

Once on the cavern floor, Michael exited the chair. Immediately he could see their six inch sample hole from the day before. And there, less than twelve inches below the ice, lay their discovery. Michael was in the middle of taking measurements when Bill's satellite phone began to ring.

"Hello," Bill answered. "Oh, it's you Mr. Hackman. Yes, I know we were supposed to wrap up yesterday, but we had one more sample we had to finish. You can be assured there will not be any additional costs for this extra day of being on site."

Bill was so engrossed in his conversation with Mr. Hackman, he couldn't hear the sound of a Tomcat snow transport heading his direction. The sound of the gas powered winch had drowned it out. This eight passenger caterpillar vehicle belonged to the Japanese crew posted in the next section. They knew this was Bill and Michael's last day and had traveled over to say their farewells.

Before Bill could stop them, they were over the cavern. "I'll talk to you later Mr. Hackman!" Bill slammed the receiver on the phone while frantically trying to get the surveyors to stop their vehicle. But it was too late.

Below the surface, the vibrations fragmented the walls and ceiling of the cavern. At first, snow-like particles floated from above. "What's going on up there?" Michael radioed to his partner.

Suddenly particles turned to ice cubes, which turned into sheets of ice descending on Michael. He covered his head attempting to shield himself from the onslaught. A huge piece of ice struck him on the back of his head knocking him unconscious. When he awoke, he was encased in an avalanche of ice, and could hear the sound of his air pack timer ringing in his ears. The shrill noise meant he only had five minutes before the air in his tank would be depleted!

"Help me, Bill," was all Michael's weakened voice could get out. In response, all Michael could hear was the ringing. And it seemed to get louder.

Unexpectedly Michael sat up, in his own bed! His heart was racing a mile a minute! The telephone on the nightstand was ringing, just like the sound of his air pack.

Becky lunged across the bed toward the nightstand. "We're you having that nightmare about Alaska again?" she inquired while reaching for the phone.

All Michael could do was nod his head while exhaling in relief that it was only a dream.

"Hello, Hansen residence," Becky answered. Her tone abruptly changed from one of sleep detriment to one of anger. "Bill, do you have any idea what time it is? Just because it is only 11:30 in California doesn't mean it is in the rest of the world! For your information, it is 1:30 in the morning here in Kansas City. I have a good mind to hang up on you right now!"

Before she could proceed any farther, Michael reached over her shoulder and plucked the phone from her hand. "This better be important pal, or we're both going to be in trouble." The minutes ticked away while Michael listened to his fellow archeologist. Leaning back against the headboard, he rolled his eyes to the ceiling in an attempt to calm his wife's disgust. "I'll call you back in the morning, Bill. Let me sleep on it."

"Sleep on what?" Becky asked hanging up the phone and turning out the light.

Michael fell back on his pillow. "Last year when I came back from that job in Alaska, I told you how Bill was claiming some great scientific breakthrough. Well, supposedly he has completed it and wants me to help test it."

Becky immediately turned the light back on glaring at her husband. "You have got to be off your rocker if you're thinking of assisting him with anything! I can't begin to count the number of times he got you in trouble with his so-called inventions during our college days. And now, with this little escapade in Alaska where he almost got you killed!"

"The man saved my life!" Michael exclaimed. "He climbed down that hole and rescued me in the nick of time.

"You wouldn't have been down that hole in the first place if he hadn't talked you into it," Becky reasoned.

Michael had no good comebacks, so silence was his best option.

"Besides, what does he have this time that is going to make him rich?" Becky asked.

"That's just it, he won't say," Michael explained. "He keeps insisting I'll have to see it to believe it. The one encouraging thing he did say, if I came he'd wire you $1,000 as earnest money. It's yours to keep regardless of whether I stay in California or not. He wants me to drive out, inspect his project, and then decide for myself whether I want to be a part of it."

Becky shook her head in disgust, flipped off the light, and turned her back to her husband as she fell back under the covers.

Michael tossed and turned the rest of the night. What did Bill have up his sleeve this time? Ten months had passed since he and Bill had completed the government job, and Michael's efforts to attain employment in his field had been unsuccessful. The money earned was consumed by past due bills and unforeseen expenses. Becky faithfully worked as a registered nurse at the local hospital in an attempt to make ends meet, but trying to raise two kids on one income was next to impossible. Feeling useless and bottled up, Michael needed to do something constructive, or he would drive his family crazy.

"If this invention turns out to be a farce, I could look around the L.A. area for employment. That way the trip wouldn't be a total waste," Michael justified as he drifted off to sleep.

The next morning Michael lay in bed while Becky drove the kids to Sunday School. His upbringing did not include any religious ties, nor did Becky's. But as conscientious parents, they saw to it that their children regularly attended church. She returned to find Michael's brown suitcase on the bed half-packed.

"I've got to give this a try, no matter how ridiculous it seems," Michael stated before Becky even had a chance to say a word.

"Fine," she snapped back. "If you think this is going to pan out, then go, but don't be surprised if it's a flop like the rest of Bill's ideas."

Michael picked Michelle and Marty up at church and told them his intentions. Leaving his family always tore at his heart strings. Michael ran his fingers through Michelle's long golden curls flowing around the soft, innocent face of his fair complexion eleven-year-old little girl.

She gazed up at him with her ocean blue eyes. "When will you be home, Daddy?"

Michael could feel a lump rising in his throat. "I don't know honey, but it will be as soon as I can." Michelle's maturity and art of eavesdropping had alerted her to the stress present at home. She knew her dad had to try something, or bankruptcy may be the only answer.

After giving Bill a call to relay his plans, Michael bid his family farewell jumping into the car. Becky stood in the driveway holding Marty's hand. She tried to restrain the six-year-old as he longed to go with his dad. Michael took one final glance at his wife. Looking past the faded blue jeans and stained sweatshirt, he saw his college bride. Her brunette spiraling hair surrounded her olive complexion complimenting her dark pool-like eyes. "This has got to work," Michael thought, "or I could lose her and my kids."

The faded yellow station wagon dotted with spots of rust wasn't much to look at, but hopefully it would make its way to California without any serious breakdowns. The 1500 mile trip would take two and a half long days. Pulling out of the driveway, he couldn't help but wonder if this was the right thing to do. Maybe Bill actually had something this time and it could be the big break they both were looking for, or maybe it was just another disappointment.

A lone streetlight greeted Michael late Tuesday night as he pulled into the drive at Bill's suburban home in Riverside. The tan colored split-level house appeared to be less than 20 years old, yet the exterior paint and yard yearned for much needed upkeep. Even in the dead of night Michael could see his friend was not concerned with the shabby guise of his abode.

Bill stepped outside the garage as Michael stiffly crawled out of the car from his tiring journey. For an instant, Michael thought he had the wrong house. "Is that you under all that hair?" Michael inquired as he neared the front door. A full black beard and mustache peppered with hints of gray embellished Bill's image. "A good barber or at least a comb could do wonders for you!"

"There's a reason for all this. You'll see." Bill's confidence level was at an all-time high as he embraced his friend.

"Well, what great invention did you drag me out here for this time?" Michael inquired.

"It's late. You'd better get a good night's sleep before I unleash this earth shattering discovery on you," Bill reasoned.

"I can't wait another night. At least tell me what this is all about," Michael insisted.

"I wouldn't be able to explain it if I had to. I'll have to show it to you, and I need the light of day to adequately do that."

Michael reluctantly spent another night wondering what in the world this project could be. Due to the length of his journey, he didn't have to worry long. He quickly drifted off to sleep. When he awoke, the morning sun grandly rose in the California sky. Now he would finally discover the essence of Bill's big secret.

The aroma of hot coffee and bacon lured Michael's long Scandinavian frame out of bed and into the kitchen.

"Good morning!" Bill cheerfully greeted him as Michael plopped down at the small metal kitchen table. After a sip of steaming coffee, he wearily forced both eyes open at the same time and groggily responded, "Morning." Silently he picked at his breakfast anticipating that Bill would burst forth with his discovery.

Bill anxiously paced the floor waiting for Michael to finish. With a bite of egg and a slice of toast to go, Bill couldn't contain himself any longer. "I told you in Alaska that someday I'd be able to prove how old this world is and how it evolved. Now I have the means to determine that."

Michael froze in mid-chew, put his fork down, crossed his arms and leaned back in his chair giving Bill one of those, "You did what???" looks.

"Follow me," Bill motioned with his arm while heading through the kitchen door to the garage. Boxes, tools and heaps of trash covered the tables and floor of the two-car garage. Michael couldn't understand how Bill could find anything in this chaotic mess. A large item covered by a gray camouflage tarp immediately drew Michael's attention. Silently and dramatically Bill unveiled the object. It resembled a long Polish sausage with shiny mirror-like panels covering the exterior with two wings folded neatly over the top of the craft.

"So you made a solar powered aircraft. That's nothing new," Michael said sarcastically.

"Those are not solar panels." A cunning smile creased Bill's face. "And I'll guarantee you there is not and never has been another craft like it anywhere in the world. Behold, the Light Assimilator!" Bill announced proudly. "The panels on the craft absorb light. Not just any light, mind you, but the ultraviolet rays of the sun. The rays work like a magnet attracting the panels to the rays. The panels absorb the rays pulling the ship along. There is no other propelling device in the craft."

Michael could visualize the buttons on Bill's shirt popping off as he finished his statement. Michael's head cocked to one side looking at Bill like he'd just told him Santa Clause existed. "And how fast will this craft supposedly go?" Michael asked facetiously.

"By theory, it should continue to absorb ultraviolet rays as long as they are out there. Consequently, it will continue to increase in velocity until it's traveling as rapidly as the rays are."

Michael's eyes opened dramatically. "You are talking about the speed of light! That is 186,000 miles per second! There is no way you can be serious about this."

Bill issued no response. Silence filled the garage momentarily as Michael's penetrating stare went from Bill to the Light Assimilator and back to Bill. "What are the wings for if you're supposedly traveling at the speed of light?"

"Conventional travel," Bill replied enthusiastically. "The wings will need to be extended for takeoffs, landings, and sub-light speed travels."

"Well, how do you determine travel speed?" Michael queried.

"The more panels activated, the faster the ship will go." With only one activated panel the ship will gain enough speed to take off and fly at 200 miles per hour. When you are prepared for light speed, the on-board computer regulates the altitude and direction. The remaining panels may then be activated and the wings will be retracted 90% allowing for just the lift needed. After that, you hold on for the ride of your life!"

"Okay," Michael said as he took a deep sigh." Let's assume this thing actually does what you're saying. What do you plan to do with it? Or do I really want to know?"

With a smirk on his face, Bill asked, "How familiar are you with Einstein's theory on the speed of light?"

Bill's implication was staggering. Michael knew enough about Einstein's work to understand what Bill was considering. "You can't be suggesting time travel! There is no way this thing could travel through time?" Bill's smug expression was exasperating. Shaking his head, Michael stormed out through the garage door. "I need to get some fresh air." Bill followed, confident of his discovery. Sounding angered, Michael turned to face Bill and asked, "If you've got this all figured out, what do you need me for?"

"Research," Bill quipped. "I need your best estimate of the earth's chronological order to date. And I need the assurance there will always be plenty of ultraviolet rays to power the Light Assimilator."

"What if it's cloudy?" Michael snapped back. "You wouldn't have sunlight to power you then."

"It's not sunlight I need. You know as well as I do, clouds have no effect on ultraviolet rays. People get sunburned just as easily on cloudy days as they do on sunny ones. It's ultraviolet rays that age us. If we weren't exposed to them, we'd live to be 1,000 years old! Now we have the opportunity to put them to good use. So what do you say?"

"I just don't know," Michael said relaxing his attitude and seriously started considering the ramifications of this project. "What determines whether you are traveling into the past or the future?"

"Very elementary, my dear Watson," Bill bantered with a smile. "We travel with the rotations of the earth for the future and reverse the rotations for the past. I know what you're going to ask next, what about when the Light Assimilator is traveling on the dark side of the earth at night? Here again, everything is under control. The craft is flown at such an elevation so that as soon as we are leaving the light of one day, we can see the light of the next. The panels will be attracted to the light rays in the distance even though we are engulfed in darkness. The centrifugal force combined with the gravitational pull will also help pull us through the nighttime. Traveling at 186,000 miles per second, and the earth's circumference measuring less than 25,000 miles, calculates into almost 8 revolutions of the earth per second! At that rate, I can travel 75 years in just one hour. As long as the ultraviolet rays exist, the panels will be attracted to them. The only problem I can foresee is if the craft was totally engulfed in water. Light will penetrate water, but ultraviolet rays will not. Rain won't be a problem because it is not a solid belt of water. For all practical purposes, the ship would be traveling above the stratosphere so weather wouldn't have an effect on it. So what do you think now?" Bill asked still beaming from ear to ear.

Still sounding skeptical, Michael inquired, "So what are you going to use this for? Discovering who wins the next World Series and make a fortune?'"

"I hope you know me better than that," Bill quipped, "but that's not a bad idea! The burning question on my mind is how this world came to be. I plan on discovering how this old earth evolved. First, you're going to help me test this baby out, and then dig up all the earthly history you can. How about it?"

"It all looks good on paper," Michael replied, "but I won't believe it until I see it."

"That's just the response I expected from you and tomorrow morning you will have your proof." Slapping Michael on the back, Bill's classic smile arched from ear to ear. "This will be my first time up in this device."

"You mean you don't know if this thing works!" Michael exclaimed! "You called me all the way out here and you haven't even tested it!"

"Don't get all bent out of shape," Bill bantered back. "It has to work. Just like you said, it looks good on paper. Trust me. Have I ever steered you wrong?"

Michael turned to respond but Bill quickly stopped him. "Don't answer that. We might be here all night." They both laughed and turned toward the garage knowing tomorrow could bring success or disaster.

CHAPTER TWO

Early the next morning, they loaded the Light Assimilator on the trailer behind Bill's old green pickup journeying into the California desert. As they rolled the craft from the trailer, Michael couldn't contain himself any longer. "If this thing does fly, where are you going?"

"Actually, I'm not going anywhere," was Bill's evasive response. "I'm going to take off and be right back."

That's all Michael could get out of him as Bill climbed into the craft. After completing a check of the instruments in the cockpit, he closed the hatch. With a thumbs-up sign, Bill activated one of the assimilator panels. The craft taxied down the dirt path and ascended into the morning sky. Michael watched as the Light Assimilator circled the area. He could vaguely see the landing gear and the wings begin to retract when the craft suddenly disappeared! Dozens of questions and fears ran rampant through Michael's mind as he stared helplessly at the cloudless blue sky. "What am I going to do if he doesn't return? There's no possible way I can explain this to the authorities. My explanation for Bill's disappearance would rank me alongside a guy who claimed he was held hostage by aliens from another planet."

Michael's eyes remained glued to the sky waiting and wondering what would happen next. It seemed like he'd been staring at the sky for an hour when he glanced down at his watch. Only four minutes had elapsed since Bill pulled his disappearing act. Out of the corner of his eye Michael caught a reflection in the sky. As quickly as it had left, the Light Assimilator reappeared in much the same airspace.

The wings and the landing gear stretched gracefully in their original position. The craft circled the landing area and softly touched down. Michael excitedly ran to the craft like a child running into the living room on Christmas morning. The hatch opened and Bill climbed out looking the same as when he left.

Michael stared at him with anticipation and asked, "Well?" Bill didn't utter a word. Acting like the cat that swallowed the canary, he reached back in the ship and pulled out a newspaper dramatically handing it to Michael. "L.A. Times," Michael read. "July 17th!" he exclaimed. "That's a week from now!"

Bill slowly shook his head up and down and stated in a deep voice, "And I was there," sounding like the great T.V. anchor, Walter Cronkite.

The entire time while securing the craft, Michael kept chanting, "It worked, it really did work!"

During their drive back to Riverside, Bill explained how he landed on the same airstrip one week in advance and walked up to the old station purchasing the newspaper. In Bill's lifetime, over 30 minutes elapsed while only five minutes passed of Michael's. Upon arriving back home, they placed the Light Assimilator in the garage and took the newspaper into the house.

"Now it's all up to you, partner," Bill commented as he collapsed into the recliner. "I need to know how old the earth really is and the chronological events leading up to today."

"That is quite a request," Michael expressed. "I could utilize my books and papers from college. I imagine Becky could box them up and mail them here, but I wouldn't mind seeing her and explaining in person what is going on."

Bill, knowing Michael needed Becky's blessing to continue on his project, insisted he drive home to get the necessary material. Michael hung his head shamefully and admitted, "We're getting a little desperate for funds right now. That $1,000 you wired Becky was nice, but it will take more than that to get us out of the hole. Is there any way you could lend us some cash temporarily?"

"I've got a few bills of my own I need to get cleared up," Bill started to say as his voice faded away into another dimension. Then that familiar cunning smile appeared on his face, and Michael knew Bill had some wild plan up his sleeve. "Toss me part of that newspaper," Bill requested as he quickly sat up in his chair. "Let me know if you come across anything of interest."

Bill examined the front half of the paper while Michael perplexingly took the sports section. "There was an attempt on the President's life last weekend, I mean this next weekend," Bill discovered.

"Do you think we should warn them?" Michael asked as he looked up from the sporting section.

"We shouldn't do anything to change the future or the past. Besides, no one was hurt in the incident," Bill concluded.

They read until Michael stated, "You know the heavyweight boxing title bout coming up at Caesar's Palace this weekend? Well, the challenger won in a split decision. He had been quite an underdog at 10 to 1 odds."

"What do you mean - had been?" exclaimed Bill. "He still is the underdog at 10 to 1 odds and we're going to take advantage of it! I can probably scrape together $5,000.00. You're going to take it to Vegas tomorrow and wager it all on the challenger. After you pick up the $50,000.00 in winnings, head over to Kansas City and pick up your family. The money will provide the extra cash to cover your debts and to bring the whole family out here for the rest of the summer. There's plenty of room. Besides, I know your work efficiency will be greatly improved if your family is here."

"We can't do that!" Michael rebutted. "That's illegal!"

"Now what's illegal about it?" questioned Bill. "It's perfectly legal to wager money on anything in Vegas."

"But I don't believe in gambling," Michael contended.

"It's not gambling when you're 100% sure of the outcome." An impudent smile flashed across Bill's face. "I've always wanted a sure bet and this is it. It's not like we're trying to get millions, just enough to get us through until we go public with the project."

Michael obstinately agreed. It was Bill's money to do with it as he pleased. Michael was certain if he had refused to place the bet, Bill undoubtedly would have driven there himself. Phoning Becky, he disclosed his plan to come back and get her and the kids for the rest of the summer. Promising to bring some extra funds, he told her to notify the landlord of their intentions. He didn't want to reveal to her the purpose of Bill's project over the phone knowing she would consider him too insane to return home. He also failed to mention his little detour through Las Vegas.

Saturday presented itself as another beautiful southern California day. Michael apprehensively headed for Kansas City via Las Vegas with a pocket full of money. He was as nervous as a long-tailed cat in a room full of rocking chairs walking up to the wagering window at Caesar's Palace. The $5,000 stuffed in his pocket weighed him down like a gold bar. He felt as though all eyes in the palace were staring at him as he placed fifty $100·bills on the counter to wager on the challenger. Taking a deep breath, he gave the teller his bet. She calmly counted the money and handed him his receipt. Cautiously glancing around, Michael folded the receipt, stuffed it in his pocket, and turned to exit the Palace.

Las Vegas presented itself as an entirely new experience for Michael. The lights of the casinos in the early evening lit up the strip like Christmas. The glare of neon flashed in his eyes at every glance. Even the McDonalds glowed with an abundance of colorful lights in an attempt to lure the occasional hungry gambler down on his luck. The next four hours crept by as he circled the strip taking in the sights. Walking the streets, he observed a variety of people going to and fro along the busy strip. The people's dress ranged from T-shirts and blue jeans to tuxedos and furs. Rich and poor alike stood next to each other while pursuing their dreams with the one-armed bandits.

At last the time to collect the winnings arrived. Cars streamed out of Caesar's Palace as he rounded the corner. Entering the Palace he thrust his hands in his jeans pocket to retrieve the receipt. Fishing through his front pockets only revealed a paper clip and loose change! Hurriedly he put his hands in his back pockets only to find his billfold.

His trembling fingers sorted through it quickly, but he was positive he hadn't placed the receipt in there. Searching his mind for a possible clue, he remembered a stop at McDonalds to get a bite to eat. Frantically, he headed towards the Golden Arches. "What am I going to do? Bill scraped together his last dollar for me to place this bet. I don't even have enough funds left to get to Kansas City."

Michael entered the restaurant on a half-run heading for the counter. "Did anyone turn in a winning receipt from the fight at Caesar's tonight?"

In return, he got a response, "If we had found it, we wouldn't give it to you."

Returning to where he had been sitting, he searched the floor. All he could find was a dried-up pickle and a cold, dirty French fry. The last remaining possibility was the bathroom. The search there came up empty. Leaning over the sink, he didn't know whether to bash in the mirror or cry. Desperately he tried to remember what on earth he could have done with the ticket. His boggled mind swam in confusion with everything that had transpired. Slowly, he looked up at himself in the mirror and noticed a small corner of a piece of paper protruding out of his shirt pocket. His heart skipped a beat as he reached two fingers in and pulled out the folded receipt. Exhaling, he looked up. "Somebody up there must like me."

With the ticket clenched tightly in his fist, Michael entered the Palace. Nearing the window he wondered what else could possibly go wrong. Much to his surprise, everything went smoothly. The challenger won the split decision just as the paper had indicated. Michael pocketed the $50,000 and warily headed for his car. Adrenaline pumped through his body at such a level he knew he couldn't sleep. Hopping in the wagon, he continued his trip to Kansas City. Driving straight through the night, he couldn't help but wonder what he was going to say to Becky and more importantly, what her response would be. The only evidence he had to show her was the $50,000 from Vegas. Why hadn't he brought the newspaper along to verify his story?

Late Sunday evening Michael rolled into the driveway hungry and fatigued. Greeting the family with hugs and kisses, Michael was relieved to be home. He was also exhausted having been up the last 48 hours. Becky had a thousand questions, but she could tell he wasn't in the mood to talk. By the time Becky had the kids tucked in; Michael had collapsed on the bed. She lovingly pulled his shoes off tucking him in for the night.

Michael woke up the next morning to find Becky lying beside him, staring. "I suppose you want to know what's going on with Bill." He sat up hanging his feet over the edge of the bed. The time had come to level with his wife. When he mentioned the words "time machine" Becky threw her hands up in a fit of rage.

"What are you doing wasting your time with that crazy nut? I should have known better than to let you go see that lunatic!" Michael sat on the corner of the bed until she quieted down. He began telling her about the incident with the newspaper as he walked over and fished the wad of bills out of his suitcase. After finishing the fight story, he tossed the cash in her lap. Becky unfolded the tax receipt and read aloud, "From Caesar's Palace in Las Vegas, Michael Hansen, $50,000!" Stillness filled the room as Michael awaited her response.

Slowly she rose from the bed to look her husband straightforward. "You expect me to believe this ridiculous story to cover up the fact you've been gambling in Vegas! It doesn't matter what scheme Bill has devised or if you just happened to hit the big one. I don't like it! Wagering on this fight had better been Bill's idea because if I find out you instigated it, you'd better pack the remainder of your bags now!"

Michael left the room without saying a word. Becky's feelings were understandable. There was no way of reasoning with her in that state of mind. Besides, he had nothing to reason with. He had been just as skeptical when Bill presented him with the situation. Going down to the den, he started packing the books he needed to take to Riverside.

Minutes later, Becky appeared at the doorway. "And what do you think you are doing?"

"Bill needs me to research the history of the earth before he starts his journey back in time," Michael responded stoutly tossing a book onto the stack near the door.

"So you're sticking with the time machine story," Becky quipped back. "Well, I'm not that gullible!"

Snapping back, Michael rebutted, "You don't have to believe me, but I'm going back with or without you. I'll be leaving at 1:00 P.M. sharp!" He watched Becky storm from the room leaving him with his books.

Shortly after that intense discussion, Michelle's head poked around the corner. "Come in honey. What are you doing out there?" His daughter stepped into the room with a look he'd never seen before on her tear stained face. After a lengthy hesitation, the child leaped into his arms clinging to his neck.

"Are you and Mom going to stay together, Dad?" Michelle sniffled with crocodile tears running down her cheek.

Michael peeled her arms from his neck in order to lean back and see her watering eyes. Remorse squeezed at a vulnerable spot in his chest. She'd heard part if not all of the heated conversation he'd experienced with his wife. "Don't worry honey. Everything is going to be all right." Kneeling, with his hands on her shoulders, he looked into her enormous tear-filled eyes. "Daddy needs to go back to California for a while to help Bill."

"Please Daddy, can we go too?" Michelle pleaded.

"You'll have to talk to your mom about that," Michael replied as he returned to his feet. With his daughter's help, he completed packing the material needed for the project.

Upon completion, Michelle grabbed her dad's hand. "Let's go talk to Mom together."

Michael feared another confrontation with Becky and didn't want to argue in front of Michelle. As they rounded the corner of the hallway, Michael stopped in his tracks. At the end of the hall were Becky, Marty with his teddy bear in hand, and three packed suitcases!

"We're ready whenever you are," Becky stated quietly. Michael sensed a veil of mist forming in his eyes. His chin began quivering as he forced a whispered "Thank you". Becky ran the length of the hall and into his loving embrace. "I'm sorry I ever doubted you," she sobbed. "I'll gladly follow you anywhere, even if this is a crazy idea." Michael, too choked up to respond, repeatedly blinked as a joyful tear ran down his cheek. Michelle and Marty joined in to form a family hug. For that moment, they were one big happy family. As Michael's head rested atop his wife's shoulder, he couldn't help but wonder what lay ahead for this family in the next few weeks and especially what lay ahead for Bill Abrams.

Becky remained quiet during the trip to California while the kids bubbled over with questions wanting to visit Disneyland and Universal Studios. Michael tried to explain how work came first and his responsibility for helping Bill, but he ultimately promised to do what he could to show them the sights.

Bill heaved a sigh of relief when the Hansen family arrived. He too had had his doubts whether Becky would accept the situation. Bill was especially glad when Michael handed him the cash. After they had unpacked, Bill announced he was going downtown to the bank and asked if anyone would like to go along. After hinting at promises of ice cream to all good little boys and girls on the trip, Michelle and Marty quickly jumped at the opportunity.

As soon as the door swung shut behind them, Michael located the newspaper Bill had obtained the week prior and showed it to Becky. Before she'd even had time to digest the significance of the newspaper, Michael grabbed Becky's hand and led her into the garage. Uncovering the Light Assimilator, Michael tried to explain what it did and how it did it.

Becky never indicated what she thought of the machine or if she believed it worked. Grabbing his head between her hands, she looked directly at him. "Do you plan on getting inside that thing?" Michael shook his head in denial. "Good," she said with a sigh of relief. "Then your work has my blessing."

Becky's response was good enough for Michael. He and Becky agreed it would be best if the kids weren't allowed in the garage in order to avoid the obvious questions. Michelle and Marty would be informed of the situation at a later time.

CHAPTER THREE

The next two months Michael studied more books and internet articles than he had since college. Every scrap of information readily available to answer or logically hypothesize Bill's questions piled high on Michael's table. When Michael thought he had accumulated all the information he could acquire, he and Bill sat down in the living room to digest the data.

"I know I'm putting you on the spot, Michael, but I need to know the chronological age of the earth?" Bill asked.

Taking a deep breath Michael responded, "Most scientists will tell you the earth is millions, if not billions of years old. Their diagnosis is based partially on facts and partially on logic. From a logic standpoint, we know the earth had an Ice Age, some form of a devastating flood in most areas, and the whole earth shows signs of being tropical at one time. During the 5,000 years of written history man has not indicated any significant changes in their living conditions. Therefore, we assume these physical changes occurred gradually over millions of years."

Bill leaned back in his chair tapping a yellow pencil on the table. "I don't care what other scientists think. I want to know what you think."

Michael proceeded, "I have reasons to doubt the world is billions of years old. There are grounds to believe catastrophic events occurred, and the changes were not gradual. Example: We know our oil developed from fossil fuels, mainly dinosaur oil. Millions of these enormous reptiles roamed the earth at one time to create the oil reserves we have today. For some reason, the majority of them died at the same time and in the same areas. The grease from the carcasses pooled together seeping into the ground. There it chemically reacted forming today's oil and gas deposits. Science has proven that newly formed oil reserves will keep their pressure for 20,000 years and then dissipate into the surrounding rocks. If dinosaurs became extinct millions of years ago, why do oil drillers still strike pressurized oil pockets which shoot their oil skyward? The pressure should have dissipated hundreds of thousands of years ago."

Bill was so engrossed in Michael's report, he never heard Becky enter the room to bring them a pot of coffee and plate of cookies. She leaned over his back setting the tray on the table. Bill's startled reaction kicked the bottom of the table scattering the plate of cookies on the floor.

"A little jumpy?" Michael chuckled.

"You would be too if you were about to try what I have set out to accomplish," Bill rebutted picking up the cookies. "Michael, that statement is implying that dinosaurs would have lived in the last 20,000 years. You and I both know from our studies that dinosaurs and man did not live at the same time."

Michael, holding his index finger up in the air to silence his partner responded, "Then how do you explain this!" Michael handed Bill a series of pictures. "These came from Glenrose, Texas. A few years ago a movie was filmed there called "Footprints in Stone." In the Paluxy River basin, they discovered a number of fossilized three toed dinosaur tracks. Alongside those tracks were a number of human footprints. And in one case, the human stepped into the dinosaurs track. They had to be fossilized at the same time!"

"Oh, some prankster just carved those in there to make us wonder," Bill quipped back.

"I don't think so," Michael responded. "They chiseled out a couple of the footprints, cut through them, and discovered the mud was compressed under the footprint ruling out that possibility of them being carved in at a later time. The one thing I can't understand is why some of the human footprints are 18 inches long!"

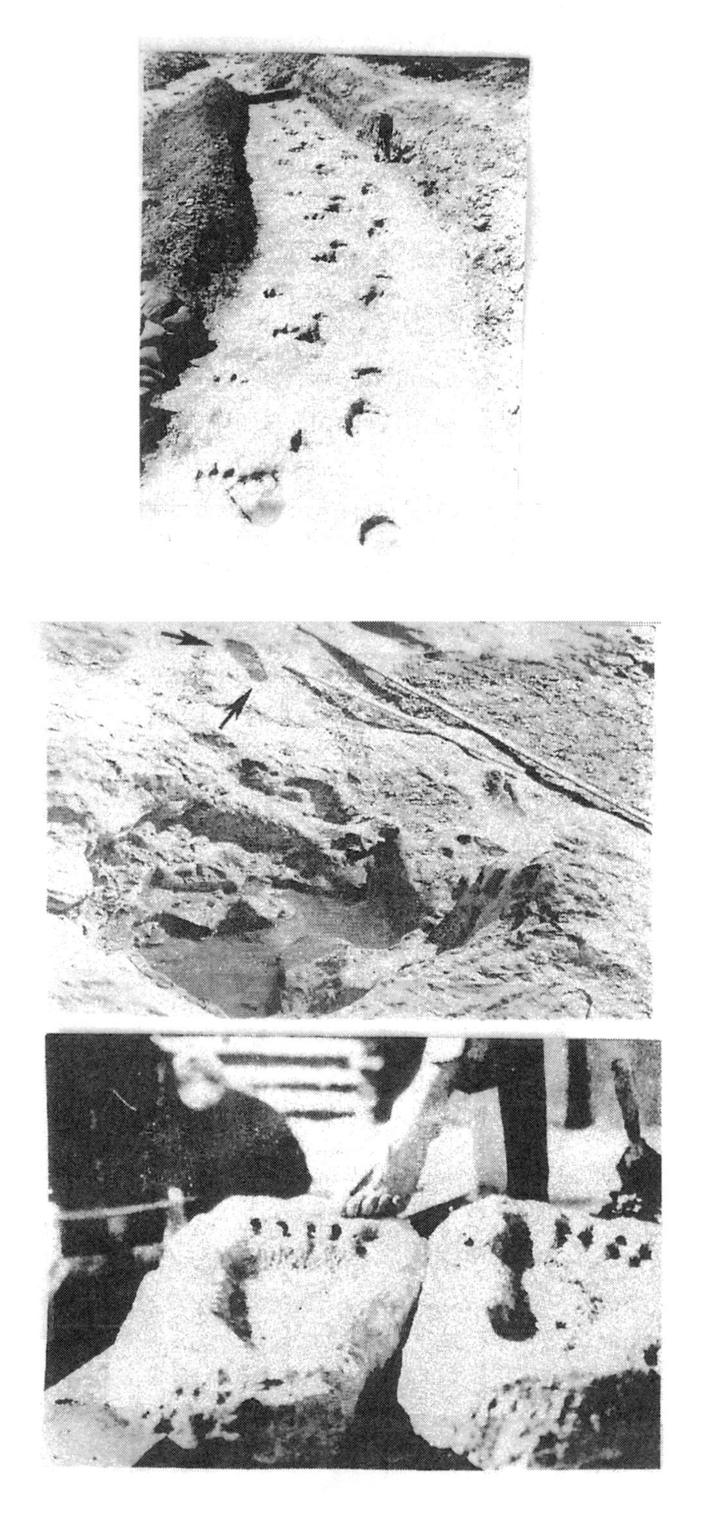

Michael paused for a moment allowing Bill to interrupt, "If I recall correctly, most dinosaur fossils date back to be millions of years."

"No way," Michael rebutted. "As you know, anthropologists use two primary tests for gauging the age of their finds: Lead Age and Carbon 14 Dating. The Lead Age method measures how much radioactive uranium has converted into radioactive lead. Unfortunately, there is always ordinary lead in the article that does not originate as radioactive uranium. It is figured in the calculations making the item appear to be ancient. Also, the fact that radioactive uranium can be washed away by water over the years before it has a chance to convert to lead makes the procedure very questionable.

"Carbon 14 Dating works somewhat similarly. While plants and animals live on the earth, they absorb radioactive carbon from the sun. When the life forms die, they lose half of their radioactive carbon every 5,600 years. When a bone is unearthed, science determines how much carbon is left and how much it should have absorbed when it was alive. From there, anthropologists work backward to calculate how long ago it lived on the earth. The only problem is the fact that the sun may not have been emitting the same amount of radioactive carbon as it is now. And if the world were completely tropical at one time, a much greater quantity of carbon dioxide would have been ingested by the plant life. One inaccuracy I see with the results of Carbon 14 Dating is that most articles either test less than 10,000 years old or over a million! Why the big gap?" Michael questioned.

Bill pondered that as Michael continued, "Let's look at a method of dating the earth by studying the rivers. At the end of each river lies a delta. A delta grows each year from the sediment flowing down it. I studied what I felt were the two oldest rivers in the world, the Nile and the Mississippi. For each river, I took into consideration that over the past 100 years more sediment has been deposited due to advanced cultivation practices. Still, each river dated to be approximately the same number of years old, between 5,000 and 7,000. To have a river delta millions of years old, imagine a major river ending in southern Georgia with Florida being the delta. If the world is millions of years old, then something has happened to change all the river systems we now have.

In studying the river bed charts, I found where a continental shelf exists below the current ocean levels. The river beds continue until they reach the old shelf as if the oceans levels were lower at one time."

Michael continued on. "Another way to date the earth is by our geo-clocks. Look at Niagara Falls or Horseshoe Falls. They have been eating rock away from the riverbed for centuries. It was first measured in 1641 by the French explorer, Hennipin. Gauging the current rate of erosion gives us a maximum lifespan of 7,000 years for that landmark."

"Here's another example why man and dinosaurs may have lived together at the same time," Michael said while passing Bill another photo. "In the Havasupai Canyon in Arizona they have discovered pictographs of dinosaurs and other modern creatures together. You would think the artist would have seen the animal to be able to draw it. And this has occurred countless times across the globe."

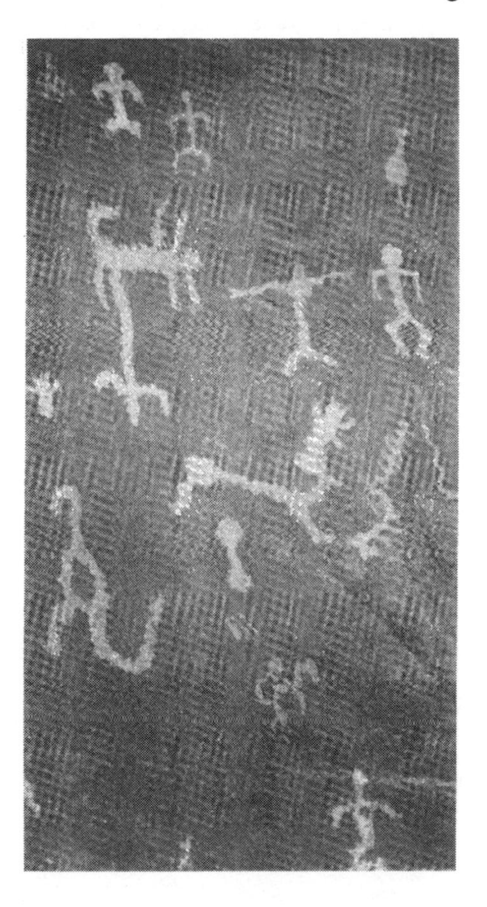

Bill loved it! If the world weren't millions of years old, then he would not have to travel back as far in time to witness history. "Go on! I want to hear more." Bill listened intently as Michael listed other possible reasons for a sudden catastrophic change in the earth's condition. Bill knew he could travel 75 years per hour. At that rate, he could travel 1,800 years in a day. If he had to go back ten million years, it would take him almost 15 years to get there. But to go back only 10,000 years would take a matter of days! Bill was liking the sound of this more and more as he prepared to ask the next question on his list.

"Now hold on a minute," Michael contended. "I'm not talking origins of the earth here. I'm talking catastrophic changes that altered our planet from a tropical haven to what we have today. Let me give you one more puzzling example," Michael said while shuffling through his papers. "Do you remember when we took half a semester studying the prehistoric arthropods called trilobites? Those little marine creatures looked like huge cockroaches with exoskeletons to protect them. They looked like centipedes walking on the bottom of the ocean. Most of them ranged from two to four inches long and could curl up like a centipede when threatened. They numbered in the millions in the first inch of the fossil record on top of the pre-Cambrian void. Supposedly they became extinct during a global catastrophe 250 million years when 90% of all marine life was wiped out. Well, here's a picture of one that had been killed, stepped on, by something wearing sandals!

"Now, either civilized man is a lot older than we first thought or these little creatures lived in recent history. I am beginning to believe that man, dinosaurs, and even trilobites lived together on this planet surrounded by a tropical haven until something catastrophic happened." Michael was grinning from ear-to-ear just waiting for Bill to urge him on.

Bill sat back in his chair. "Okay, I'm ready. Now let's hear it!"

Taking another deep breath, Michael started on a theory that could rewrite all of the history books in the world. "You and I both know from our studies in Alaska that the earth was entirely tropical at one time. The permanent ice caps sit upon a tropical haven of quick frozen alligators, saber tooth tigers and a variety of other animals including a very intriguing camel." Michael paused to see if he would get any reaction from his friend. After a moment of silence, he continued. "Do you remember in college when Professor Berman told us about a frozen herd of mammoths discovered in Siberia with tropical buttercups still in their mouths? And you, in all your wisdom, confronted our loved professor on how a herd of mammoths could be frozen while eating tropical plants. Berman tried to convince us they wandered out on a frozen pond and fell through. You couldn't leave it alone. You replied, "Sure, and I just walked here from Mexico City this morning." That one got you kicked out of class for three days."

"Okay," Bill contended. "Enough of the reminiscing. Let's get on with your speculations."

"The earth probably rotated in a perfect circular orbit around the sun instead of an oblong orbit like it is now. More than likely, the earth rotated on its magnetic axis."

"But that would have cut back the number of days in a year!" Bill interrupted.

"Precisely!" Michael looked at Bill encouraging him not to butt in so quickly. "Did you know there are some early calendars indicating our original year only had ten months? Remembering your Latin, what numbers do Sept, Oct, Nov, and Dec represent?"

Immediately Bill piped in, "Seven, eight, nine and ten."

"Correct," Michael responded praising his pupil. "What months are September, October, November and December on our calendar today?"

With a puzzled look on his face, Bill answered, "Nine, ten, eleven and twelve."

"A Roman King, Numa Pompilius, in 713 B.C. added January and February to the beginning of the calendar when he was advised by his scientists that the calendar was off," Michael proudly announced. You could tell by Bill's reaction, it got his attention.

Michael continued with his theory. "Before this catastrophic event, without the extreme seasonal changes, many more species of plants and animals existed. We also know that somewhere between the tropical era and now, the earth experienced an excruciating Ice Age. Animals were quick-frozen in a tropical climate without a chance to escape. That does not point to a gradual cooling. We also proved the ice encasing those specimens was not salty. I doubt that it originated from our oceans. And you and I both know the pole regions are the most arid regions of the world because storm systems normally do not flow over them. We also discovered the numerous lakes of the northern U.S. and Canada were not formed by glaciers but the earth being pulverized by something." Michael prepared for his knockout punch, and Bill was ready for it.

"Comets, like Halley's Comet, are made of ice. The tail we see behind the comet consists of ice particles dissipating from the comet. It was a dud when it came past in 1986, but according to history, it was spectacular in 1910 and more dramatic each time before that. That would tend to make sense since the comet is getting smaller all the time. Can you imagine the size that snowball would have been 10,000 years ago?

"The rings of Saturn are made of ice. The sun shining through the ice is what gives it a rainbow effect. There are theories that a comet made a close pass to the planet and the magnetic makeup of the planet trapped the ice in an orbit around Saturn. The rings are gradually moving away and will someday escape its gravitational pull.

"Also imagine what would have happened if that comet and the earth had a close encounter of the icy kind. Vast amounts of ice particles would have been attracted to the magnetic poles of the earth. Some of these particles may have been miles in length, leaving crater-sized indentations at their points of impact. Remember how our study of the ice cap revealed that the Ice Age glaciers went as far south as Iowa on the States side, but barely touched Siberia on the other side of the globe. The epicenter of the Ice Age was near Magnetic North Pole!"

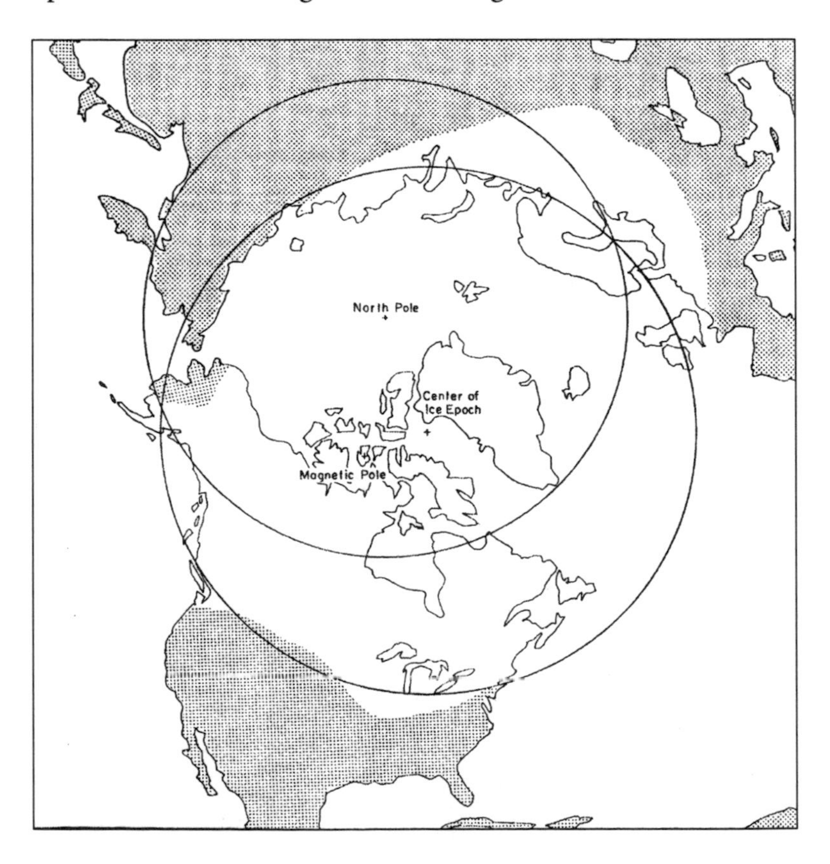

Michael's buttons on his shirt were popping as he continued, "Any life in those areas would have been covered in a massive rain of ice. The earth would have been thrown onto a different axis, throwing the oceans out of their beds onto the dry land and devastating everything in its path. The earth would have been knocked out of its circular orbit to its current orbit. The impact would also explain why the earth is 27 miles shorter through the poles than it is through the equator." Michael went on to explain the changes this would have made on the earth and how this theory fit the scientific record.

"And this clears up the whole global warming phenomenon," Michael summarized. "It is true that glaciers and our ice caps have been retreating for hundreds of years, but not because the temperature has gradually been getting warmer, and definitely not from carbon emissions. It is because the ice was not native to this world. The ice will retreat to a point of equilibrium in relationship to the average temperature of the earth."

Michael could tell Bill was not focusing on what he was saying and had boldly gone where no man had gone before! "Hey!" Michael shouted. "What planet are you on?"

"I'm right here on earth," Bill contended. "Just a different time than you are!"

"Okay," Michael smiled back at him. "Can you give me a couple more minutes?"

Bill nodded his head up and down trying to center his attention on his friend.

"Do you remember when Professor Berman told us about the formation of the Grand Canyon and how the Colorado River took millions of years to cut a path over a mile deep in solid rock to create the canyon?"

"Yes," Bill replied. "I think I recall hearing some controversy about that lately."

Michael continued. "The main argument against the gradual erosion of the Grand Canyon is the fact that the Colorado River enters the canyon region at 2,800 feet above sea level and leaves the plateau region at 6,900 feet!

In my research, I read a book called Carving Grand Canyon by Wayne Ranney and some works by Dr. Walt Brown. It looks like the water draining from my newly deposited ice caps formed two huge lakes, Grand Lake and Hopi Lake at the head of the canyon region. These two lakes extended over four states; Utah, Colorado, New Mexico, and Arizona. The water pressure got so high that it broke through a land bridge on the southwest side of the lake. Millions of tons of water funneled through the canyon draining both of the lakes. The fresh sediment that had been thrown out of the ocean beds when the comet struck was quickly eaten away forming the canyon we see today.

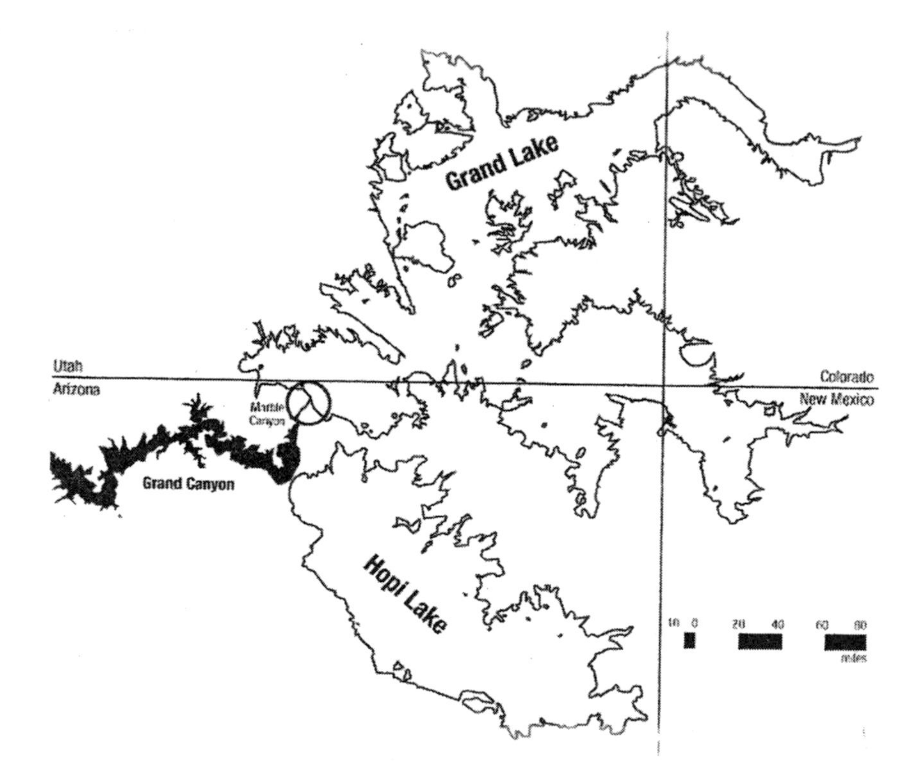

By this time, Bill had heard enough. He was dreaming of ice falling from the skies on the north and south poles. He remembered Michael saying the ice did not fall on the central sections of the earth. Supposedly, guiding his ship around the equator would keep it safe from the falling debris. To be sure, Bill directed that question towards him.

Michael confirmed his belief and added, "If the earth is knocked out of orbit, your ship should stay locked on the equator."

"This next question will be a tough one," Bill said leaning forward putting his elbows on the table. "How long ago did all of this happen?"

"That is a good one," Michael responded. "There's no real way to know exactly, but my best guess is approximately 7,000 years ago. The earth may be millions of years old, but this is the catastrophic event you're looking for. Anything that lived before this event cannot be Carbon 14 dated correctly due to the drastic change in conditions. And I can't find any geo-clocks on earth that date over 7,000 years old."

"This is great!" Bill exclaimed. "You have performed your part of the project better than I ever imagined. As far as I'm concerned, all systems are go. I'll be ready to leave first thing Monday morning."

"Now wait a minute, Bill. I could do years of research on this subject. I don't want you zooming off half-cocked expecting to find dinosaurs in 7,000 years and then blaming me when you don't," Michael responded.

"At this point, it wouldn't matter what other information you organized and presented to me. I'm ready to discover the past!" Bill concluded.

Knowing Bill was going to do what Bill wanted to do, Michael decided to ask some questions of his own. "How far back do you plan on going?"

Bill retrieved his calculation tables. "I can travel 1,800 years in a 24-hour day. I'm planning on traveling for as long as I can, maybe up to 24 hours. After stretching my legs, I will go another 12 hours or so. At that rate, I should be back to your Ice Age in a few days."

"Do you plan on conversing with any of the people you may encounter?" Michael questioned.

"Some," Bill reasoned. "Hopefully I will be able to acquire the proper attire for the era I will be visiting. I'm planning on taking my entire library of language software. Theoretically, I should be able to converse with anyone I meet. But my best language is my parents' native Hebrew."

"Where do you want to go and what do you want to see?" Michael continued his questions.

Bill leaned back in his chair for a moment scratching his head. "I'm not too interested in the immediate history of the world. Most of it has already been well documented. I wouldn't mind seeing the construction of the pyramids, the Great Wall of China, or Solomon's Temple. My great-Grandfather was a Jew from the old country. He painted some vivid pictures in my memory of the Holy City of Jerusalem. Palestine is where I feel the most comfortable trying to converse with people."

They went on into the night discussing plans and possibilities. The contagious excitement engulfed Michael too as he expressed his desires to go. Bill convinced him it would be too much stress on Becky and-the family. "Once we've proven this is a safe and simple procedure, you'll be the next to go," Bill promised.

The time had come to celebrate. Bill uncorked a special bottle of wine saved for an occasion like this. They toasted each other, the project, and the Light Assimilator. When they both had their fill, they raised his glasses in unison and proclaimed, "Let there be Light!"

CHAPTER FOUR

The next day, to further celebrate, they indulged the kids with a trip to Disneyland. Throughout the day, Michael tried to relay to Becky the extent of Bill's aspirations and what the game plan entailed. Michael and Becky decided the time had come to let the kids know about the project. Michelle had grown frustrated because no one would answer her questions concerning this great mystery.

Sunday morning, as usual, Becky drove the kids to Sunday School. When they arrived home, the overhead garage door was open as Bill and Michael busily loaded the Light Assimilator with supplies for the journey. Bill packed his 35mm Nikon, digital camcorder, books, maps, rations, extra clothes for different time periods, and other supplies for survival in the wild. He even stowed his .38 revolver with plenty of rounds, just in case.

Bill allowed the kids to climb all over the craft. Marty had an especially good time sitting in the cockpit behind the flight wheel pretending to be a fighter pilot. Michelle alertly noticed there were no motors or jets on the ship. Her dad tried to explain that its power came from ultraviolet rays.

"What are ultraviolet rays?" she asked wrinkling up her freckled nose.

"They are rays emitted by the sun," Michael replied. "Bill says if we didn't have the ultraviolet rays we'd live to be 1000 years old!"

"Oh, you mean like Methuselah," she quipped back.

Puzzled, Michael turned to his daughter. "Who's Methuselah?"

"The Bible says he's the oldest man that ever lived," Michelle factually replied. "He lived to be 969 years old. But that was a long time ago, before the flood. We learned about him in Sunday School this morning."

The kids continued to examine the craft until lunch. Following the meal, the men persistently reviewed their checklist to make certain Bill would have everything he could need. The mechanics of the ship were checked and doubled checked to assure everything functioned properly. The left side of the cockpit contained the gauges used for conventional flight. The right side had been revamped to house the onboard computer, chronologer, and other time travel instruments. A battery powered refrigerator and storage space for dry goods filled the space directly behind the passenger seat. The power pack regenerated during flight, but had a hand crank attached, just in case. A pressurized 10 gallon stainless steel water tank sat strapped to the base of the wall behind the pilot's seat with a hose-like drinking spout attached to the side of his seat. A crawl space, back in the tail section allowed further room for supplies, spare parts, tools, and clothing.

The reclining captain's chair with folding armrests enabled the pilot to rest comfortably during long durations of travel. A flotation device under the seat would also double as an in-craft pillow. An elaborate first aid kit rested under the passenger seat. The loaded .38 tucked itself away in a pouch on the back side of the pilot's seat.

Blastoff was scheduled for mid-morning. Bill went to bed early and tried to rest before his journey began. He tossed and turned most of the night dreaming of discovering the lost civilization of Atlantis and its many secrets. When the Ice Age came, the levels of the oceans rose dramatically, and the civilization drowned in a sea of water, submerged forever.

Michael couldn't sleep. Something Michelle said bothered him. Getting out of bed, he wandered into the study and flipped on the light. He searched the study until he located the book he wanted. Walking over to the desk, he sat down, switched on the reading lamp, and started thumbing through the pages.

The sun peeked over the horizon as Bill arose from his restless sleep. Walking towards the kitchen, he noticed a light in the study. Peering around the doorway, he saw Michael at the desk; face down in a book, asleep. Going to the kitchen, he returned with a steaming cup of coffee. Placing it in front of Michael, he lightly tapped him on the shoulder. Sleepily, Michael opened one eye then the other while sniffing the aromatic coffee. Extending his arms up in the air, he stretched the kinks out of his back exhaling an enormous yawn.

"What have you been doing?" inquired Bill.

"We need to talk." Michael stood, grabbed the hot cup of coffee, and started walking toward the window not looking at Bill. "I think you should consider postponing your takeoff for a couple days."

"Do what!" Bill shot out of the chair he had settled into. Grabbing Michael by the shoulders, he wheeled him around to face him. "The equipment is in perfect working order and so am I! You and I have gone over every feasible complication! What's the problem?"

"I have found a possible time in history when men lived to be over 900 years old," Michael contended. "Maybe they weren't exposed to the concentration of ultraviolet rays we are today."

"And where did you come up with this new unfounded information?" Bill inquired angrily.

Picking up a book on the desk, Michael handed Bill his grandfather's Jewish Torah. Confused, Bill gaped at it momentarily. "The Bible! I didn't think you believed in fairy tales, Michael? Next you'll be telling me to watch out for Thor and the Forces of Darkness!"

Michael bristled. "My job is to find any possible problems with the intensity of ultraviolet radiation during the history of the earth. I just discovered this last night and I haven't had a chance to check it out."

"Let me hear what you've found." Bill sat down in disgust. Michael could tell Bill was letting him explain this just to patronize him. "During the first ten generations of life in the Bible, men lived to be over 900 years old. Then came the flood and life spans 'quickly declined to what they are today. It doesn't state why, or at least I haven't discovered it yet."

Calmer now, Bill tried to reason. "You and I both know the Bible was written many years ago by people attempting to explain their feeble existence. During the early years, they thought it would be best if men lived a long time. That way they could populate the earth more quickly. Besides, look at the example of the Ark; how could a man with primitive tools possibly build a seaworthy structure capable of carrying two of every creature? You know as well as I do, the whole thing was not logically possible. A few hours from now I will have the knowledge of what actually did happen. Don't make me wait another day. I don't think I can stand the suspense any longer."

"I don't believe in this religious stuff anymore than you do. But this indicates things were different at one time. I feel responsible for you on this journey. I wouldn't be able to forgive myself if something went wrong," Michael reasoned.

"Your assignment was to evaluate the scientific history of the earth and provide me with a possible evolutionary timetable. You have done an excellent job of that. I didn't ask you to decipher all the mythologies of the world! Let's forget about this silly idea and go launch that rocket."

"You're the boss. But I'd still prefer if you'd wait a few more days and let me examine this further," Michael said.

"If there was something further to uncover in the Bible, someone would have discovered it by now," Bill contended.

"You never said that about my cornet theory," Michael spurted back.

"Okay. Lighten up," Bill reasoned. "We're both a little edgy today considering what is going to transpire. Let's relax and get ready to go."

Michael didn't respond as he walked out of the study. Bill's confidence could not be wavered, and Michael realized there was nothing he could say that would change his mind. It didn't take long to rouse the others. Soon they were on their way to the desert crammed in Bill's old green pickup pulling the concealed Light Assimilator on the trailer.

"When will your first stop be?" Becky asked.

"I thought about going back to the day Julius Caesar was executed, but it will be nearly impossible to stop on the exact day when I'm traveling that distance. I may stop at Old Jerusalem first and see the Temple. I'll be lucky if I can get within a week of any particular day, so don't wait around for me after I leave. When I return to this era I want to make sure and overshoot my departure. I don't think it's a good idea to come back before I leave." Their chuckles helped relieve some of the tension filling the pickup. The butterflies of anticipation held all involved captive as they neared their destination.

As they unloaded the craft from the trailer, Bill reminded Michael not to wait in the desert for him. "It may be a couple weeks before I return. When I'm traveling a week at a time the computer will gauge my re-entry for me, but when I'm traveling years at a time I have to re-enter manually. One thing I'm not sure about is the coasting factor. When I travel at the speed of light for an extended period of time, I may coast a few days on reentry. Trial and error will determine the length of time for that. In the meantime, you have the keys to the house and the money in the cookie jar."

Michael looked at Bill and asked the question that had been plaguing him. "What should I do if you're not back in a couple weeks?" His voice cracked at the end of the question as he stared at the ground circling his foot in the powdery dust.

Bill stepped forward, gave him an awkward hug, patted him on the back, and reassured him, "You know I'll be back. I don't want you to have all the fun with the $50,000!"

Everything was set. After kissing the kids, Bill walked over to Becky, grabbed both her hands, and in a reverent voice said, "Thanks for the support you've given Michael during the project. Without his help, I wouldn't have gotten off the ground."

Michael's digital recorder silently captured the events in the morning stillness of the desert. Bill climbed in the Light Assimilator, double checked all the controls and closed the hatch. Within minutes, the craft taxied down the dirt road and lifted off into the sunshine-filled morning sky. The kids cheered as Bill made three loops around the area and with the ship angled in a southerly direction towards the equator; the landing gear and the wings began retracting. In the blink of an eye, the craft disappeared into nothingness. The children's cheering softly died away. Only the faint sound of the recorder remained breaking the silence of the still desert air. Finally, Michael lowered the camera as the Hansen family stood arm-in-arm on the hot desert road staring into an empty blue sky.

After what seemed an eternity, Michael interrupted the silence. "We'd better go now."

"Will Bill be back soon?" Michelle asked peering up at her father.

"I hope so," was Michael's only reply. Last time Bill had returned by now. Michael kept reminding himself that it would take longer this time. However, Michael had an uneasy feeling that something was wrong, and all he could do was sit back and wait.

CHAPTER FIVE

Obscure scenes of light streaked past Bill as he rocketed around the equator of the earth. At 7 1/2 revolutions per second, the difference between day and night was indistinguishable. The date chronologer, his instrument for measuring time, spun backward rapidly. Bill's first test of time travel approached. Dr. Hans Eikman of Germany theorized if man could travel back in time, he would not be able to survive before the date of his existence. In five minutes, Bill would be nearing the date of his birth. He held his breath as the final seconds ticked away to his birthday. With a loud expulsion of air, the date passed and Bill breathed a sigh of relief.

The years rolled back as Bill remembered events in history. He pictured the tragedy of 9/11 when September 2001 turned over. He didn't want to think about the explosion of the Challenger space shuttle disaster in 1986. That situation hit a little too close to home. In 1963, he visualized President Kennedy's assassination. When 1955 rolled up, he thought of the birth of rock-n-roll and the King, Elvis Presley. The dreadful day of December 7th at Pearl Harbor came to mind when the chronologer gauge read 1941. In 1936, he recalled Jessie Owens winning four gold medals in front of Hitler at the Olympics in Berlin. At that point, Bill considered taking the craft out of light speed, but his goal was to solve the mystery of the existence of the world. There would be plenty of time to witness these historical events after this mission was accomplished. By now, the years involving World War I were on the screen. As the turn of the century approached, Bill pictured Teddy Roosevelt and his Rough Riders charging up San Juan Hill. When

1865 appeared, Bill considered the magnitude of the Civil War and the assassination of Abraham Lincoln at Forde's Theatre. "What would have happened to the U.S. if John Wilkes Boothe had been stopped before firing that fatal shot?" Bill pondered as he sped backward through time. He knew he had the power and the knowledge to stop Boothe. He also knew that any interference would change the total course of history. He had to keep telling himself that in no way could he do anything that may change the events of the future.

By now the chronologer had whirled back to the late 1700s. George Washington would be attempting to lead a new nation. The plight of Washington's army at Valley Forge and the many battles fought and won even though he was out-manned and out-gunned would be a thrill to behold. The midnight ride of Paul Revere and the signing of the Declaration of Independence transpired as he streaked headlong around the earth.

Reviewing these dates in history helped time pass more quickly, as if it wasn't passing fast enough! Bill reached back for his Hebrew language book to do a little reviewing. The Hebrew he had learned in his early years wasn't bad, but he thought it might be a good idea to brush up. The first stop he computed for 60 A.D. to check out the Temple in Jerusalem. He was sure he'd be ready for a break after 26 hours of time travel.

The next time Bill took his nose out of his book, the chronologer rolled up 1500. As 1492 became visible, Bill couldn't help but see the historical parallels of his journey and that of Christopher Columbus. Bill's intentions included discovering facts and taking them back across time to people interested in knowing the true reality of the past. He dozed off thinking of Columbus's journey and his experiences with the people of the new world. Bill was awakened a few hours later, not by his ship, but by his biological needs. Planning ahead, he had installed his very own porta-potty which he replicated from those used by the astronauts. He could have disengaged from light speed, set the craft down, done his duty and taken off, but that would have wasted 15 minutes. And those 15 minutes translated into about 20 years of travel! A smile spread across Bill's face as he recalled one of Becky's pet peeves about the male gender. "Men, you know how guys are about not wanting to stop when they're on the road!" Besides, the danger of stopping and being discovered was always risky.

Relieved, Bill decided to check out the kitchen. Digging into his rations, he found a variety of edibles. The refrigerated compartment behind the passenger seat contained fresh fruits and cold cuts. Other foods, ranging from jerky to granola bars, were packed away in boxes in the storage area. The pressurized water tank provided an adequate amount of fluids available at his disposal. Numerous packs of red licorice and bubble gum to chew on filled one whole sack. "This should keep my mouth busy for the trip," he said aloud. He paused for a moment. Those were the first words he'd spoken since he'd engaged in light speed. "Testing, one ... two ... three." The words seemed to wobble as he spoke'. Bill opened his mouth and vocalized a sustained high C note. It sounded beautiful. He finally had the natural vibrato he'd always wanted!

As Bill finished lunch, the first century approached. Before long Bill would attempt his first re-entry into the distant past. A knot began forming in his stomach as he considered the possibilities of something going wrong. The anticipation of this monumental historical event overwhelmed him. One hundred A. D. presented itself on the chronologer. In order to see the Temple, he had to wait until 70 A.D. or before. The Temple was destroyed at that time by the Romans and never rebuilt. "Another 30 minutes should do it." The minutes passed by at a snail's pace. Bill checked and rechecked the output information on the computer screen. All systems were running smoothly.

Finally, the time came for his first encounter with the past. Bill prepared to measure the coasting factor during re-entry and set his instruments for October 1, 60 A.D. "October in Palestine should be good sleeping weather for this weary traveler."

At the prescribed moment, Bill engaged the re-entry program and held on like a child on his first merry-go-round ride. The shades of light streaming past the ship began changing colors. The differences between day and night became distinguishable as the craft slowed down. With wings extended and only one light panel activated, Bill slowed to earth-time. The sun's beaming essence peaked over the eastern horizon. It was the start of a new day, but what day? The instruments registered September 21st. It had taken ten days to coast out of light speed even though it took him only ten seconds.

The next order of business involved trying to decipher where in the world he was. The instruments located him on the equator and 20 degrees Latitude West. Bill quickly examined his charts. "I should be smack-dab over the Atlantic." Sure enough, looking out the window he could see an ocean of water below him. Bill set his course across Africa towards Palestine. Bill charted his route, lowered the altitude, and took a leisurely tour over the untamed continent. Unbelievable herds of zebras, giraffes, and elephants meandered throughout the African terrain. Bill shook his head in amazement. In less than 2000 years a scene like this would not exist because of man's greed and carelessness. The craft flew over an enormous village. When this curious silver bird was spotted, dark-skinned people ran out of their huts shaking hand-pruned spears at it. He knew they would interpret this vision as a sign from their gods. To avoid any further confusion, he decided to raise his altitude.

Moments later the sand dunes of the Sahara Desert dotted the horizon. Bill unrolled his modern-day geographic maps of the area. After computing the needed calculations, Bill circled the desert. The western loop discovered some interesting findings which he began compiling in his notebook. "In 60 A. D. the total size of the Sahara Desert is only two-thirds of that currently recorded. The modern day expansion of the desert must be an ongoing process. At this rate, the desert will be nonexistent by 3000 B.C. This also means unless our climate conditions change, the desert could take over Northern Africa by 2500 A.D."

While Bill considered the impact of his discovery, what appeared to be gleaming mountains emerged on the eastern horizon. Bill's eyes widened in expectation. Before him materialized one of the Seven Wonders of the Ancient World, the Great Pyramids of Egypt! The original inlaid limestone majestically encased the upper half of the pharaoh's tombs. Bill considered landing for a closer inspection, but after further deliberation, he decided his next jump out of light speed might condone a more opportune time frame. "Maybe the Egyptians would be in the middle of constructing one of the monstrosities during my next stop in time," Bill thought. He left the glistening pinnacles in the background and proceeded to fly across the Sinai Peninsula to Israel.

Circling the Dead Sea, he beheld the fortress of Masada. In just a few short years, 1000 Jews would hold out against the Roman army for over a year. The Romans finally penetrated Masada by building a ramp to the top of the mountain. Then the invasion force, using a gigantic battering ram, smashed down the gate only to find the inhabitants had committed suicide rather than be taken captive.

Straight ahead lay his destination. It was time to find a suitable and non-populated place to land. Bill steered away from populated areas to prevent detection, yet he wanted to get as close to Jerusalem as possible. A mile south of the city spread a flat flood plain adjacent to a range of rolling hills. A low pass of the area found no large rocks or crevices to hamper his landing. A composition of sand and dust created an adequate runway. Bill circled one more time making his final approach. The dust flew up behind the craft as the back wheels touched the surface. Easing the flight controls forward, the front wheels of the ship bounced down on the sandy soil of Palestine. One hundred meters later, the Light Assimilator rested at the edge of the Hinnom Valley.

Popping the hatch, Bill raised his nose in the air, inhaling the Middle East atmosphere. The fresh and pure morning air seemed to vitalize Bill's desire to explore the region. He quickly started to exit the craft when his tired muscles told him they'd been sitting in one position for too long. Laggardly, he crawled from the cockpit and planted both feet on the ground. "Mother earth still feels the same. Too bad I can't say the same for myself." Five minutes of calisthenics loosened Bill's tight muscles and prepared him to discover Jerusalem. He quickly changed into a robe and sandals depicting the era. Hoping to get a few choice shots of the Holy City and the Temple, Bill grabbed his camera hiding it under his robe. The Light Assimilator sat next to an embankment. Unfolding the gray camouflage tarp, he spread it over the craft. "Hopefully it should be safe for a couple hours," Bill remarked as he started to walk away. He hesitated as he checked his inside pocket for his Hebrew language book before climbing over the hill on a small dusty path leading in the direction of the city. In anticipation of his journey into the past, Bill had allowed his hair, mustache, and beard to grow. His Jewish heritage showed in his physical features. Bill knew he was taking a chance, but this was the kind of adventure he loved.

The walk to the city took longer than Bill had anticipated. Either the distance was farther than he estimated or walking on a rough, sandy path in leather-tied sandals slowed him down. He reasoned it was probably the latter as he approached a well-trodden path leading to the city's southern gate. His heart skipped a beat when he looked up to see two men walking towards him. "Should I say anything?" Bill questioned as the two men approached. He reasoned a first conversation would be safer here rather than inside the crowded walls of Jerusalem. The men were nearly passed when Bill gathered his courage. "Shalom."

Without hesitation, the two men returned the Hebrew greeting. Bill felt as if he had passed his final college exam. His pace quickened in anticipation walking over the final knoll. At the crest, he froze in his tracks. There, atop the next hill, majestically appeared the Holy City of Jerusalem. Little did her inhabitants know that in six short years she would be under siege, and four years later totally destroyed by the Romans. Bill's emotions welled over him as he gazed at the ancient city. After overcoming the shock of this reality, Bill pulled out his camera and snapped a few shots of the impressive scene. Quickly, he slid the camera under his robe and continued down the dusty path to the open entrance.

Roman Centurions patrolled the gates of the city. Israel, currently under the rule of Caesar, kept Rome busy with their various religious disputes. Confident of his disguise, Bill approached the entrance. No one spoke to Bill as he passed through the portal. He tried not to laugh after a close-up look at the guard's attire. He'd forgotten about the skirt-like uniforms the Centurions wore during those times. The skirts and red plumes down the middle of their helmets reminded him of the rock bands in L.A.

Unfortunately, Bill had forgotten his map of the layout of the old city. "There shouldn't be a problem making a loop around the city, but I need to remember exactly which gate I entered." Straight ahead Bill saw the Pool of Siloam. Bill recalled his grandfather's story how King Hezekiah back in 700 B.C. drilled a tunnel through solid rock from the Gihon Spring in the Kidron Valley to inside the city walls. It provided fresh water for his people in anticipation of an inevitable attack from Assyria. The pool sparkled as Bill helped himself to a drink of cool, invigorating water while rubbing elbows with dozens of the local inhabitants. Many women gathered around the well with their clay jars to draw the daily water for their families. These five gallon vessels would be filled and placed on their heads to transport the water back to their homes.

He continued on his way toward a long walled alley. The walkway stretched a quarter of a mile ahead of him in the direction of the Temple, so Bill followed it. The walls on both sides stood four feet high and made of the same type of stones as the walls surrounding the city. Off to the right, Bill saw what appeared to be a large arena. The oblong structure rose two stories and was shaped in an oval like a stadium enclosing a football field. He wanted to peek inside, but the doors were braced shut. His disappointment was short-lived as he caught a glimpse of the edge of the Temple courtyard.

Bill's pace steadily quickened until he froze in his tracks as he rounded the entryway to the courtyard. Before him, in all its grandeur, stood the temple. All the recollections handed down from his grandfather could not begin to describe this historic structure. He backed up into the shadows of the entryway, glanced around to see if he was being watched, and pulled out his camera. Quickly he snapped a picture before concealing his camera back in his robe. He couldn't risk being discovered. If exposed, he'd surely be crucified by the Romans.

The courtyard bustled with activity as Bill strolled closer to the Temple. Sacrificial doves and lambs became bartering tools for the money changers as Jews came from all over the land to worship their God. Gazing up at the Temple, he could see why the Romans left no stone unturned when they destroyed it; the seal between each stone sparkled from the essence of pure gold. Bill's hypnotic stare spanned the massive structure marveling at the 100 foot Corinthian columns in front of the Temple. Suddenly, he felt a tap on his shoulder. Startled, Bill jumped back. Much to his relief it was only a merchant trying to market his wares. The merchant held up a wide gold bracelet in one hand and a silver beaded necklace in the other and surprisingly spoke in a language Bill did not recognize! Shocked, Bill shook his head and cautiously backed toward the gate. Hurrying through the entryway, he paused to lean against the wall. His heart raced a mile a minute, pounding wildly against his chest. "The merchant must have been speaking Greek," he puffed. Greek was an acceptable language in Jerusalem during this time. Bill's dying confidence convinced him to leave the over-crowded city.

CHAPTER SIX

At approximately 2:00 P.M. Jerusalem time, Bill exited the city on the east side. The next sight to meet his eyes brought a sickening feeling to his stomach. On a hill, less than 100 meters away, a group of Roman soldiers were in the process of executing two people by crucifixion. As Bill walked closer, he could see the two men were still alive. He didn't want to see anymore, but his feet carried him toward a small crowd gathered around the foot of the two crosses. His unwilling gaze fixed upon the two men agonizing in the hot sun. Apparently they had hung there the majority of the day. Massive pools of blood below the crosses appeared brown and dried from the sun's radiant heat. Wounds from the large rusty spikes no longer bled profusely. The men hung forward on their crosses gasping for air. In order to breathe, they pushed themselves upright against the painful spikes in their feet. After an agonizing breath they slowly drooped back to their hanging position. "Why are they here and what have they done?" ran through Bill's mind, but his fear restrained him from asking anyone. He overheard talk of alleged conspiracy and innocence. Anger started to fill Bill's heart as he watched these fellow Jews being wrongfully persecuted, but there was nothing he could do. He couldn't help but remember his grandfather's depiction of the crucifixion of the great teacher, Jesus. In the next ten years, the Romans would run out of trees executing the Jews. Then they resorted to nailing their victims on the city walls! Tears filled his eyes as he realized these people were his ancestors, yet there was nothing he could do. Grabbing his wrists, he too could feel the burning pain of the jagged spikes penetrating his flesh.

Suddenly, a soldier grabbed a long rod and placed it in front of one of the convicted men's legs and behind the cross. He slowly pried backward as the knee hyperextended. The man screamed out in pain as his knee cracked and broke. The other man soon experienced the same excruciating pain as the soldiers attempted to make the men die sooner. Without the ability to push themselves upright, the men could no longer breathe. Bill couldn't take it any longer as the men gasped for breath in agony. He numbly stepped backward through the crowd inadvertently backing into a woman. Stunned by what he'd witnessed he spoke in English, "Excuse me". The woman and several other people stared at him in confusion. In desperation, Bill turned and ran from the crowd. In his jumbled state of mind, he ran northward around the curve of the city wall. Checking to see if anyone was in pursuit, he saw no one. Relieved, Bill walked the path past the northern road to the city that led to Galilee.

Once Bill calmed down, he realized the pangs of hunger were gnawing at his stomach. Spotting a fig tree off to the side of the road, he decided to try a few. Picking up a hand full of freshly fallen figs lying in the grass under the tree, he sat down on the ground leaning against the tree trunk popping one into his mouth. "Not bad," he remarked with a look of approval on his face. "But anything tastes good when you're hungry."

By the shadows around him, Bill realized he was now on the north side of the city. He could also tell approximately four hours of sunlight remained before his ship's power source would rest over the horizon. Originally, he had planned to spend the night in this region, but now seeds of doubt had planted themselves in the back of Bill's mind. He knew he needed to circle the city to reach the south gate where he had entered. No way would he return in the direction he had come. That was a sight Bill never wanted to be confronted with again. After his fill of figs, Bill started on a loop skirting the city wall away from the crucifixion.

Around the next bend, the outer wall of the Temple courtyard came into view. To his left, a picturesque garden full of beautiful shrubs and blooming plants fronted a hill laden with groves of trees. Bill sat in the garden area for several minutes trying to remember the layout of the map he had left in his ship. "This must be the Garden of Gethsemane and behind me lies the Mount of Olives. The scenic backdrop would make a beautiful picture." Bill got his camera out and removed the lens cap. The Temple created a majestic backdrop for the garden setting. Bill backed up to obtain a wider shot of the area with further intentions of scaling the Mount of Olives for an overview of the Garden of Gethsemane. Focusing his camera, he alertly heard a twig snap off to his right. There, less than 50 meters away, a Roman Centurion marched right for him.

The huge soldier barreled toward him. "Halt!" in Hebrew. Bill froze in his tracks. In a split instant, he had to make the decision of his life. If he stayed, there would be no way to explain his camera. If he ran and was caught, he'd probably be decapitated on the spot! The approaching Centurion was only 20 meters away. Knowing it was now or never, Bill turned and ran as fast as he could toward the Mount of Olives. The Centurion yelled to his comrades for assistance giving Bill the opportunity to distance 100 meters between them. But he knew his lack of knowledge of the area could prove fatal. Immediately, he ditched his camera and language book in a hollow log. "If I'm captured I will play the part of a deaf mute and maybe they'd let me go."

Along the shrub-laden hillside, a number of caves dotted the Mount of Olives. If he couldn't outrun them, maybe he could hide out until his pursuers tired of their search. Making sure he'd lost visual contact with the guard, he darted into the shadows of a nearby cave. From his vantage point, he watched the soldier appear with two others at his heels. They split in three directions and began searching the area. Bill could do nothing but wait.

It seemed like hours passed without seeing neither hide nor hair of the guards. Each minute spent in the dark and dingy cave wasted valuable sunlight. At last, he poked his head out in the fading light of day to make sure there weren't any soldiers in sight. Sneaking back to the hollow log, he retrieved his camera along with his book. Crouched low, Bill cautiously crept from shadow to shadow along the rocky hillside making his way through the olive trees. At the edge of the grove, running to the south, the Kidron Valley meandered around the outskirts of the city. "The valley must run close to the area where my craft is parked. As long as I maintain sight of the city and the countryside, I should be able to keep my bearings. If only I hadn't forgotten my map in the ship."

Bill slid down the embankment of dry powdery dirt and sand. From the depths of the Kidron Valley not much could be seen. Occasionally Bill climbed out of the valley surveying his progress. Relief washed over him when he recognized the south gate. With less than an hour of sunlight left, the fastest way back to the ship was the path he had initially traveled. A quarter of a mile south of the gate, Bill reached the path he had entered the city on. Looking back at Jerusalem, Bill saw two guards standing near the gate. "They can't be the same ones I avoided earlier." Following the path to the top of the ridge he turned around for one last glimpse of Jerusalem. His gaze didn't last long because as soon as he turned he noticed two Roman guards coming towards him! "The Roman guard that spotted my camera must have informed every guard around the city!" Bill kicked up clouds of dust as he sprinted over the hill. Clenching his side, he branched off the main path and headed down to the ship. Bill couldn't keep up this pace much longer. The combination of the heat, his attire, and sandy soil made running nearly impossible. Gasping for air, Bill stumbled along hoping to reach his destination soon.

Only half of the sun's beaming essence remained on the horizon as his camouflaged craft came into view. "If the sun sets too far there won't be enough rays to get the ship airborne!" Bill ripped off the tarp and unlocked the hatch, quickly stuffing the tarp behind the seat. Only a four or five minute lead separated him from sure disaster. "If I get caught now, you may as well write me off as history," he commented as he hopped in the cockpit. In the shadow of the adjacent hill, the Light Assimilator slowly rolled around the base of the hill with the majority of the panels activated. "Please, let there be enough light," Bill pleaded nearing the edge of the embankment. Only one-quarter of the sun remained as Bill rounded the hill. "Hopefully that will be enough," Bill questioned as his ship turned toward the remaining sunlight. The Light Assimilator accelerated down the path just as the two soldiers appeared over the ridge. They froze as they saw this strange contraption accelerating directly towards them! Immediately, they turned and hightailed it back to Jerusalem as fast as they could while Bill's craft lifted off into the sunset over their heads.

The lack of sunlight prevented the ship from immediately reaching light speed, but Bill was thankful just to get out of that place. He set a course toward the setting sun, gradually catching up with the huge fireball. The ship angled south to the equator as Bill readied the craft for the jump to light speed. Bill activated the remainder of the panels and sped once again into the wild blue yonder of the unknown past.

Hunger and fatigue overwhelmed the traveler when he had a chance to sit back and relax. His feet throbbed in pain. Removal of his sandals revealed numerous broken blisters which developed during the day. After some medical attention, food became the next order of business as he rummaged through his rations to choose his menu. "It has been a very long and tiring day," Bill uttered as he finished his meal. He then recalled the only sleep he'd had during the last 24 hours was the few times he'd dozed off in the craft. That thought brought on an enormous yawn as Bill reclined the seat and settled in for a long winter's nap. The current date registered 407 B.C. "Another 1,000 years or so of rest should do me well," Bill thought as he dropped off to sleep.

CHAPTER SEVEN

Twelve hours of hard sleep revitalized the weary time traveler. Bill awoke 900 years earlier, rested and refreshed. Opening his log, he recorded the vivid events of 60 A.D. Bill spent the day reading, listening to his music, and playing computer games. While snacking on a variety of munchies, the chronologer rolled up 2200 B. C. "I think I'm due to get out and stretch my legs," Bill remarked putting his food and log back in their respective places. "Maybe I can catch one of the great pyramids under construction," Bill commented as he studied his date charts using a strawberry licorice twist as a pointer. "The larger pyramids have already been constructed, but they might be working on a smaller one now."

The time had come for the second chapter of his land adventures. Activating the reentry program, he coasted into history again. This time he chose 2225 B.C., a beautiful spring morning in the month of May. The instruments registered 70 Degrees West on the equator. Bill checked his maps to confirm his position should be over South America. Looking down, his mouth gaped in confusion. "There's nothing but ocean down there! Something must be wrong with the instruments." Circling the area, he scanned the instrument panel for any possible malfunctions and eventually headed east in an attempt to locate land.

At 35 degrees West, the welcomed sight of land appeared on the horizon. It resembled the west coast of South America, but his maps indicated he should be in the middle of the Atlantic. What looked to be the Amazon River seemed a logical reference point, so he followed the meandering river to the east. It flowed to the eastern edge of the continent and turned south with another land mass on the other side. The giant river made a perfect outline of the east coast of South America and the west coast of Africa!

"I'll bet the land masses are all together! Michael had alluded to the possibility of continental drift. That's how the faraway lands were easily populated. Won't he be thrilled to learn his theory was correct! But neither of us thought it would have occurred this late in time."

Bill's quest for knowledge of the earth's origins began to unfold. He jotted down his findings in his log and considered taking photos of the area, but he knew pictures of the river wouldn't prove anything to anyone. "There will be more conclusive facts later for me to take back to the modern world."

He turned the ship towards the desert and the wonders of Egypt. Decreasing in elevation, he looked for the giant herds of wildlife observed on his previous trip. Much to his surprise he found only remote groupings of animals. Then it dawned on him he hadn't seen any signs of man. He was contemplating the reasons for this when he noted he should be approaching the Sahara Desert. For miles, lush green grass stretching in all directions covered the futuristic desert floor. Finally, rolling sand dunes appeared in the distance. Flying over the sand he registered another reading of its size to compare with his last trip. He knew the desert should be smaller than before, but when it measured less than 200 miles across he was shocked! More facts raised more questions. Shaking his head in disbelief, Bill wrote down the information. Unbeknownst to Bill, this was the start of a long list of unanswered questions that would fill his log before his journey was over.

In the distance, the glimmering limestone peak of the great Cheops Pyramid appeared. In order to set the craft down and get a close-up look at one of the Seven Wonders of the Ancient World, it was imperative to find an unpopulated area close to the pyramid. This task proved mysteriously easy as he couldn't find anyone within a 50 mile loop of the site!

Landing the craft within a mile of the great shrine, he prepared for a little sight-seeing. The hot, dry air jolted his system as he opened the hatch. Placing his sandals back on his already sore feet, he crawled outside. After engaging in some exercises and partaking of one last drink of water, he grabbed his camera and jaunted off to hunt down and shoot a pyramid. It felt good to stretch his legs even though the pain in his feet felt like his sandals were lined with sandpaper. Sand and grass intermingled across the countryside. Bill noted how the sand seemed pebbly and not fine like typical desert sand.

The sight of the great Cheops drew him straight ahead. From this distance, he could see the pyramid's limestone covering encased the surface from top to bottom. Over the years, the majority of the limestone covering would be chipped away by robbers or excavators looking for a secret entrance to the pyramid. Bill knew photographs of this spectacle would be concrete evidence of his presence in the past. The burning question in the back of his mind remained, where are the people? He checked over his shoulder repeatedly, certain that someone would be coming soon, but each time his glance caught only the lush grass waving in the hot desert breeze.

Further to the east should be the Great Sphinx. The exercise would do him good, so Bill turned from Cheops and headed east. The sun's oppressively hot rays beat down on Bill as the wind swirled mercilessly from the west, stinging his exposed skin as he approached the area where the nose-less Sphinx should be located. Ahead, a mound of sand appeared with a rounded rock protruding from the top. Encouraged, he picked up his pace until he could see it wasn't a rock at all! Rising above the encroaching sand stood the head of the Sphinx! Bill recalled his Egyptian history, remembering the body of the Sphinx was covered with sand when Napoleon discovered it in 1798. It had been theorized that its nose had been removed gradually by kids striking it with sticks when the face rested at ground level. Bill walked around to the front of the Sphinx. The nose and the face emerged in perfect condition without signs of wear or damage. But most surprising, the headdress and face were painted! The headdress was a brilliant yellow and dark blue, while the markings around the eyes were highlighted in black. "Wait until Professor Berman sees a picture of this," Bill said as he backed up to get the shot. The nagging question of the sand ate at him the more he thought about it. This desert isn't currently large enough to create a sand storm of the capacity needed to cover the Sphinx. And why does it appear to be ocean-like sand?" The unspoiled face of the Sphinx shimmered in the noonday heat as he pondered these questions. Without a good answer, Bill trudged back to his craft to resume his journey.

Reaching the ship, he questioned his failure to locate some inhabitants of the day. He flew over the banks of the Nile, assuming the Egyptians would be living on the fertile plains of the river. Again, no human life could be found, but an abundance of animal life flourished along the river. The meandering Nile graced the valley supplying needed moisture for the animals and foliage. Retracing the same path he had taken his last trip, he found the countryside greener than before, but still unpopulated.

"Certainly the Jerusalem area will be populated," he said as he angled toward the location of the Holy City. The Jordan River stretched northward before him to the site of the city, but surprisingly nothing but a mound of dirt and rock existed. Out of desperation, Bill turned the ship to the east towards one of the oldest known civilizations on the earth, Babylon.

Once the plush valleys of the Tigris and Euphrates rivers were in sight, a pleasing smile spread across Bill's face. Below him, villages filled with people dotted the plain. He could understand why people inhabited these fertile plains, but why only here? He had previously covered thousands of miles of terrain with no visible inhabitants. Now, within a few miles, dozens of villages and hundreds of people populated the area.

On the horizon, the top of an enormous building rose above the countryside. A large city spanning the plain on the northern edge of the Euphrates River surrounded the colossal structure. "This is probably Babylon," Bill remarked as he circled the city. On the edge of the city, the unfinished ziggurat towered above the city. Normally these pyramid-like temples were 20 to 30 feet high, but this one rose a hundred feet into the clear blue sky. Bill had seen ziggurat-like structures the Inca Indians constructed in South America. Unfortunately, due to their clayey brick construction, they didn't stand up to the test of time.

Consequently, a great monument like this can be easily destroyed or will waste away with the seasons. Bill zoomed in with his telephoto lens and snapped a few good pictures of the overwhelming structure as he looped the area. Determined to find some other people on the earth, he continued eastward on his trek.

The population of people dwindled quickly as Bill left the Mesopotamian Valley. The snow-covered peaks of the Mountains of Tibet appeared refreshingly new, undaunted by time or man. Swinging south to Southeast Asia, Bill found the South Pacific huddled in a small cluster of islands. These islands, including Australia, had not spread to their modern day locations.

As had been the case previously, no signs of man existed. Circling up through the Orient and then back westerly through northern Europe concluded the same results. Now he neared the English Channel, but something appeared out of place. He scanned his charts and found the northern portion of the United Kingdom angled northeasterly into the North Sea. North America positioned herself next to Europe with Iceland and Greenland nestled in the groove at the northern gap. Newfoundland fit perfectly in the Bay of Biscay, and the mouth of the St. Lawrence Seaway matched up perfectly with the Strait of Gibraltar. Yet these watery havens did not yield any signs of people. Bill circled the Great Lakes region trying to find signs of human inhabitants. Dwindling remains of a receding glacier created a flood of fresh, clear water. This sparkling water replenished the numerous lakes of the north while dissipating from the retreating ice cap.

Bill's inner time clock told him it might be a good idea to stop and take a break for a while. "Let's see what's going on in L.A.," Bill chuckled as he turned his craft towards the southwest. Before him stretched miles and miles of prairie grass waving in the vast open plains. Massive herds of buffalo and elk flashed through his mind, but no such herds existed. Only an occasional beast of the land could be spotted.

The Rocky Mountains dotted the horizon, but they did not appear as grand as he had recalled. Over the mountains, the beginnings of the soon-to-be California desert region stretched before him. Surprisingly, large lakes surrounded by lush green grass covered the majority of the flats. This sight reminded Bill more of the Everglades rather than a would-be desert. As he neared the west coast, the fertile southern California Valley appeared. Searching for a spot to set down, he noticed a level area close to the mouth of the Santa Ana River. It seemed odd to be flying over the location that would someday become Los Angeles, Hollywood, Burbank, Anaheim, Santa Ana, and Long Beach, and see nothing but rolling hills and trees.

Bill landed the ship on the plentiful grass saturating the floodplain of the river. The thought of exploring this familiar territory lured Bill to go for a short hike. Approximately two hours of sunlight remained on this beautiful spring day, so Bill decided this would be a good place to camp for the night. Sleeping in the Light Assimilator was okay, but a night stretched out under the stars in his own hometown would be interesting.

Fresh food became the first order of business. A wealth of fruits and vegetables abounded at every turn as Bill followed the river upstream. The wild strawberries, Bill's favorite, flourished along the banks of the Santa Ana. He picked as many as he could stuff in his robe and took them back to the craft for later consumption. In the river, enormous trout fought their way up the river to feed. A fishing pole was not one of the survival items he had packed for the journey, but those fish certainly did look enticing.

"If I were a cave man, what would I do?" Bill asked himself looking around the area. The light bulb came on as he spotted some small trees growing from the river's edge. Running to his ship, he grabbed his hunting knife and dashed towards the river. A straight willow limb one inch in diameter hung close to the ground. Bill cut a five-foot length and stripped the small branches and leaves from the limb. Finally, he whittled a sharp point at the small end, and his fishing spear was complete. Looking like a kid with a new toy, he bounced down to the water's edge. Bill's eyes widened as he located a large fish near the top of the crystal clear stream. With a mighty heave, he launched his spear into the water only to come up with mud on the end. Recalling his laws of physics, he remembered how water bends light. And how objects below the surface appear at a different angle than what they really are. The next fish meandering by did not escape the thrust of Bill's spear. His shot forcefully penetrated his prey. Bill held on with all his might as the fish thrashed his powerful tail in an attempt to free itself. The size of the fish made it impossible for Bill to lift his catch from the stream as his spear began to crack from the weight of his good fortune. Floating the fish to shore and picking it up by the gills, he raised the king-size trout in a show of victory. "He must weigh at least ten pounds!" (But you know how reliable fisherman's estimates are!)

Proud of his accomplishment, he returned to the ship with his catch of the day. "This calls for a picture." Bill wiped his hands off and pulled his camera and tripod out of the ship. He focused in on the fish, set the timer on the camera, and scurried to hold his catch in one hand and his homemade weapon in the other. When the camera had clicked he asked, "Now, how do I fix this thing?" His knowledge of cleaning a fish was next to nothing, but hopefully anyone can get two nice filets out of a ten-pound fish.

After Bill had cleaned up from his fishing adventure, he decided building a fire was the next order of business. The desolate beach loomed before him like the logical place for a fire, and he set out to collect the wood needed. Ample amounts of driftwood covered the coastline making the gathering quick and easy. A steep embankment on the northern edge of the beach protected a flat sandy area near the mouth of the river. Here he wouldn't be hampered by the wind if it came up in the middle of the night. In no time, a roaring fire lit up the sky as the evening sun hovered over the skyline of the Pacific, or was it the Atlantic? Either way, it produced a beautiful sunset. As the fire died down, he propped his filets over the hot coals to cook. Meanwhile, he went to the river to obtain fresh water for filling his tank. He didn't have to worry about pollutants in this water. It was the clearest and freshest water Bill had ever tasted.

Nearing the camp, Bill filled his lungs with the pure coastal air. The smell of wood smoke mingled with a slight hint of something burning quickened Bill's pace. He returned to discover his fish rather char-roasted. With a fork in hand, Bill picked beneath the outer roasted layer and gave it a taste test. "Not bad for home cooking," Bill commented placing the smoking filets on a make-shift plate he had brought on the trip. One stick of jerky to add spice to the meal, three carrots, and part of the strawberries completed his four-course meal. The moon majestically rose over the Santa Ana Mountains as Bill finished his evening meal. Bringing his log up to date, he related everything that had transpired during the day. The facts uncovered during this brief stop in time developed so many more unanswered questions. "Maybe my next stop in the past will hold the answers to these questions, or maybe it will only create new ones." Either way, Bill felt pleased about how things had worked out so far. Everything was progressing according to plan.

Bill threw more wood on the fire as darkness crept in along the beach and the shoreline. Bill stared into the rising flames as the fire's tranquilizing effect took hold. His mind raced through the events filling the last two days and what might lie ahead in the near future, which actually would be the distant past! A shiver descended Bill's spine as a cool sea breeze blew in off the rushing waves of the ocean. Grabbing his sleeping bag, Bill snuggled in for a night under the stars in the refreshing night air. Without the large city to generate heat, Southern California cooled off more than Bill had anticipated. It seemed odd not to hear or see signs of any nocturnal creatures. Come to think of it, he hadn't seen signs of any animals the entire time he had camped on the beach. The last visual contact with land animals occurred from his craft in the central states region.

Lying under the vast California sky, Bill couldn't help but think back to when his family first arrived here. He was 14 years old when his father uprooted them from his lifelong home in Brooklyn. His father, a jeweler, was a partner in a very successful business chain. Bill would never forgive his father for taking him away from his friends and the life he had in New York. His parents were also very devout Jews and tried to impose their belief on their only child. By his high school years, Bill had totally rejected their belief, which broke his parents' hearts.

Bill had put his faith in mathematics and science. There was no way he could believe in something he couldn't objectively reason or put his hands on – like the God of Abraham. Bill knew his personal mission during his college years was to prove his parents wrong. He attended

Berkeley, one of the most liberal colleges on the West coast, where he took archeological studies.

That is where he met the tall, gangly, fair skinned guy from Kansas, Michael Hansen. Bill's energy and sense of humor acted like a magnet to the soft spoken Hansen. By their sophomore year, they were dorm roommates. That was a decision Michael would live to regret on more than one occasion. The top of the list was a science experiment in their dorm room that went terribly awry. That incident brought fire departments from two stations, relocated everyone out of the dorm for two days, with Bill and Michael being expelled for two weeks!

They were best of friends until Michael discovered Becky McCallister. It was love at first sight while Bill was assigned second fiddle. Becky had just enough Irish in her to keep Michael on the straight and narrow path, and keep Bill in his place.

His senior year Bill actually concentrated on his studies and especially his senior thesis. It was worth 40% of his grade, but more importantly Bill had a point to prove about placing his mark on the science community. The title of his thesis was "Radiation Propulsion, the Energy of the Future." On paper, Bill had devised a device that would attract radiation from the sun. But to impress Professor Berman, Bill would have to prove it by constructing a working model. The metal needed was palladium, which was as costly as gold. After the metal was flattened into a six inch panel, it would need to be reverse-magnetized and clear coated. This process would cost thousands of dollars that Bill didn't have. The bank account was empty, and the student loans were gone. Even though his parents could have easily funded his education, they chose not to because of Bill's attitude toward his father and his rejection of their belief system. Bill had gone as far as even looking at Christianity just to spite his father. But both religions based their belief in Creation, which scientifically Bill could not justify. If you can't believe the first few chapters of the book, why believe any of it, he reasoned.

Eventually, it was time for Bill to swallow his pride. His father was the only person capable of providing the money needed for his endeavor. On a Sunday afternoon, Bill drove to Riverside prepared to do whatever groveling it took to get the funds he required. His mother opened the door, and Bill greeted her with a warming hug and a kiss on the cheek. Immediately, his father, shaking a boney finger at him, knew he was up to no good. It was all downhill from there. After a few heated exchanges, Bill blurted out why he came. His father threw up his hands and muttered something in Hebrew walking away toward the bedroom. Bill's mother, almost in tears, shook her head in disgust trailing him down the hallway trying to reason with her husband.

Flabbergasted, Bill had had enough. Storming out the door, he jumped in his car throwing gravel in his wake as he sped away. It would be the last time he saw his father alive.

The next day after class, Bill heard a light knock on his apartment door. He opened it to reveal his mother grasping a white envelope. Without saying a word, she extended the envelope to him. Immediately, Bill could tell by the thickness it had the cash needed to complete his thesis. But his mother wouldn't release the envelope to him! Looking him squarely in the eyes, she said, "William Benjamin Abrams, you must promise me that you will make reconciliation with your father. He has no idea I am doing this, but I know it is important to you."

Bill hated it when she called him William. And even the Benjamin reminded him of his heritage and how his ancestors came from the tribe of Benjamin. But his mother was providing the cash needed, so he swore to her that after graduation was over he would sit down with his father. The next few weeks he would be too busy completing his thesis. Besides, both of them needed time to cool off.

"Once I get this project completed, I will have done something to make my father proud of me," Bill contended.

"He already is proud of you," his mother responded. "He's just too stubborn to admit it. He's always telling me that eventually your science will prove to you what the truth really is."

That statement made no sense to Bill, but he thanked his mother for the money and promised to send an invitation to the graduation.

Bill acquired the material needed for his radiation propulsion device. He found a lab on the other side of town that would complete the reverse magnetism process. As instructed, they placed the 6 inch square panel inside a black velvet pouch locking it inside a portable safe.

To complete his thesis, Bill needed to get precise readings stating exactly how much radiation would be attracted to this size of a panel. Early Saturday morning, he carried the safe to an open grassy area on campus where no one was around. He had his Geiger counter ready to measure the flow of radiation. Ever so slowly he opened the safe. Pulling out the velvet pouch, he flipped open the top flap revealing a tiny edge of the panel. In one swift motion, the panel shot from the pouch in a beeline toward the sun! Bill's mouth hung open in amazement staring into the empty sky. All he had worked for and all his mother's money, gone in a flash. He had no readings, and he didn't even have video of the procedure. But worst of all, he had nothing to show his parents for what he had done.

Even with nothing to show for it, Professor Berman was gracious enough to give Bill a passing grade. Through all the theories and the mathematics, the professor could see potential for this procedure. As graduation day approached, Bill prepared to reconcile his differences with his father. He had two seats reserved in their name toward the front of the auditorium. The ceremony began, but the seats remained empty for the duration. Bill could not believe that his father would not attend this special event.

Following the reception, he returned to his apartment finding a message on his phone to call the local police station. After confirming his identity, they informed him his parents had been involved in a multi-car pileup on Interstate 5. "Which hospital are they in?" Bill frantically interrupted.

There was a long pause on the other end of the phone. "I'm sorry to report, Mr. Abrams, they didn't make it." The patrolman went on with the details. "It appears one car started going southbound on the northbound side of Interstate 5 causing the 13 car crash. Your folks' car was between two semis. It was instantaneous for them. Apparently, the southbound driver was high on something."

The rest of the conversation became a blur for Bill. His father believed in a loving God, and then something like this! There is no way a god would allow a tragic event like this to unfold. It just cemented the idea in Bill's mind that we are all here by an evolutionary process and everything that happens to us is strictly by chance.

Bill assumed with the torn relationship between him and his father that his parent's estate would be left to a Jewish foundation in charge of rebuilding the temple in Jerusalem. It came as quite a shock to him when Mr. Goldstein, his parent's attorney, informed him of the contents of the will. Everything, including the home in Riverside, had been left to him.

The tidy sum would have been enough for a conservative person to live out his years in comfort. But Bill wasn't the conservative type. This abundance was exactly what he needed to complete his ultimate dream. Initially, he thought he would have to patent his radiation propulsion device to get the funds needed. But now he had the resources to prove to the world the true science of the origins of the earth. It would take 12 years and most of his parent's estate to make this a reality. It was too bad his father would not get to see his grand discovery.

A tear ran down Bill's cheek as he rolled over in his sleeping bag. He eventually drifted off to sleep under the California starlit sky.

Morning arrived with a brilliant sunrise bursting over the mountains. Bill stuck his nose out of his sleeping bag into the morning air to find a rather nippy temperature to greet him. The once roaring fire smoldered to a bed of ashy coals. Unfortunately, nature called forcing Bill to exit his warm cocoon. The fresh and crisp California air raised goose bumps on Bill's skin as he ran to the ship for a jacket. It seemed odd not to see the ever-present gray, smoggy haze on the horizon. Bill could observe the distant hills clearer than ever. At that moment, his heart saddened at the thought of how pure this area is now. And then man, with all his great wisdom, enters the world and totally wasted, polluted, and destroyed the earth's vast resources.

After grabbing a bit of breakfast, he cleaned the campsite and dowsed the fire. The sun's radiant heat engulfed Bill as he went about his activities. Anxious to solve the questions that had surfaced the day before, he quickly packed the Light Assimilator. After taking off, he slowly circled his encampment. The rolling hills and fertile valleys looked so tranquil in comparison to how Bill remembered the area. Miles upon miles of city spanning the countryside flashed through his mind as he took one last look at the Southern California coast. Then he journeyed south to the equator for his next jump to light speed. "How far should I go this time?" he questioned as he activated the panels and shot farther back into the past. "With all the changes I saw this time, I'll just go back 500 years and see what this earth looks like then." Bill studied his charts as time sped by in a blur of light.

CHAPTER EIGHT

A violent shaking suddenly thrust Bill headfirst into the dash of the ship! Visions of crashing to the earth flashed through his mind while wondering what was going to occur next. Fortunately, the shaking only lasted a few seconds, but that length of time translated into a couple months on earth. While Bill contemplated what could have possibly happened, the Light Assimilator broke from light speed coasting back to earth time on its own. The instruments indicated all panels activated and operational. There was absolutely no reason this should be happening. Bill extended the wings while his heart raced gliding back to reality. Glancing down, Bill noted his chronologer registered August 9, 2351 B.C. By now his speed had decreased to 600 miles an hour with a latitude of 120 Degrees east, directly over the equator.

"The South Pacific islands should be below," he remarked as he began scanning the area. "There's nothing but land down there!" Bill exclaimed as he peered out the window. "Maybe I'd better increase my elevation and get a better overview of the area." All the while he checked and double checked the instruments. "Those vibrations undoubtedly loosened some connections inside the craft. I'm registering all panels operational, but why can I only maintain a speed applicable to conventional flight? And here I am in the middle of the South Pacific with no Pacific!" Bill's frustration grew by the minute as he leveled off the craft to obtain a better look at the region. The islands of the Pacific nestled neatly up by Southeast Asia, but there was no water surrounding them at all, just valleys of dry land! Heading west towards Africa, the ocean appeared exceedingly low.

Swinging in the direction of the southern tip of India, he found the Bengal Bay to be nonexistent. West of India, the Arabian Sea composed only half the area his maps indicated. The world had undergone some drastic changes in the last 125 years, but that was not Bill's primary concern. He desperately wanted a location to set down and restore his ship to full working order.

Saudi Arabia lay straight ahead and sounded like a good location to have a level unobstructed landing area. Lowering his altitude, he discovered Saudi Arabia to be nothing but a massive jungle! A closer examination revealed movement in the depths of the dense forest.

"Dinosaurs! There must be hundreds of them in that one small area!" Questions about what had happened raced through his mind as he continued to search for a place to land. With nothing but jungle inland, Bill retreated to the coastal areas to locate a level spot to touch down. In most places, the ocean abutted the forest leaving no possible landing options. Finally, over by the Red Sea, represented by only a wide river, he located a flat sandy area to land.

Bill spent the next four hours examining the Light Assimilator from top to bottom. Each of the panels verified as operational and properly connected. Oddly, everything appeared in working order. Confused by the developments, he sat down on the sand in the shade of his craft?" Sweat dripped from his chin as perspiration soaked his robe in this sauna-like atmosphere, yet the temperature was not excessively hot for this region of the world. "It can't be over 75 to 80 degrees," Bill said shaking his head as he wiped the sweat from his brow. It felt like it could rain at any minute, but a cloudless sky filled the airspace.

Bill stared aimlessly at his ship. Then his stare slowly returned to the sky. The horizon illumined the deepest blue tinge he had ever seen. Glancing at the sun, he noticed no painful or damaging effect from looking at the fiery ball in the sky for a prolonged period of time. Rising to his feet, he gazed into this foreign sky. "What is going on around here!" Bill yelled pounding the wing of the craft in a state of frustration. Dropping to the ground he wanted to cry, but couldn't.

From his desperation and anger arose a need to know what happened to his ship, so he reviewed the facts.

Pacing back and forth in front of his vessel, he gave this recap, "The ship, which seems to be in perfect working condition, dropped from light speed after encountering a few seconds of violent turbulence. Ultraviolet rays from the sun power the craft. The sun feels as if it is not emitting its full energy, or it is being filtered. I should not be able to look at the sun for a prolonged time, and at noonday in August near the equator we should be reaching 100 degrees. There is not a cloud in the sky, yet the humidity level is near 100 percent."

With those facts in hand, Bill determined his ship may not be the problem, but the lack of ultraviolet rays to propel the craft. "If that's the case, what is blocking or hindering the sun's rays?" he questioned aloud.

A feeling of progress encouraged him as he reached in the ship grabbing a bite to eat. "After lunch we'll take a trip up there and see what's causing the problem," Bill confidently stated while preparing his meal. Perplexing questions nagged at Bill as he finished his lunch. Packing his gear and tools, he climbed back in the cock pit.

It was mid-afternoon when the Light Assimilator arose from the sandy riverbank aiming toward the sun. Normally, the air would thin at the higher altitudes, but the external air pressure registered near constant levels. The higher he climbed, the more the prospect of his hypothesis being true became a reality. Something, glistening like a glass bubble, barred him from the sun. Finally, nearing the edge of available space, the question was answered.

"Water," Bill whispered in utter dismay. His finding answered a dozen questions and created a hundred more. Bill recalled his very words to Michael concerning a solid band of water being the one thing capable of blocking the majority of the ultraviolet rays emitted by the sun. Now, only enough rays penetrated the belt to power the ship for conventional flight. His instruments could not determine the thickness of the water belt, but this development did prove the greenhouse effect encased the earth at one time in history. "That explains why Saudi Arabia was nothing but a jungle. For that reason, the entire earth should be covered in vegetation. This environment will create perfect living conditions for the dinosaurs, and they should be ruling the earth. Animals will live in all parts of the world without the weather being a contributing factor," Bill reasoned.

He considered trying to blast through the water belt where the sun's radiation was at full power. But the water belt was located at the edge of outer space where the ozone layer is today. He knew his ship could not survive in the vacuum of space and dismissed that idea quickly.

As he accumulated these facts, the big question still remained, "How in the world did that water get up there and what's holding it up?" Without a good answer, he journeyed over Africa. A mass of trees, underbrush, and dinosaurs engulfed Ethiopia and Sudan. Stegosaurus, Diplodocus, and Tyrannosaurus Rex roamed the endless forests. Bill recorded some fantastic videos of the area as he flew overhead. His search for possible signs of man turned up empty, so he directed his craft to the north. The Sahara Desert was nowhere in sight. The panorama of a forest-laden countryside transformed into a speckling of trees as plush green grass dominated the scenery. The sun arched its way toward the western horizon. Bill could not take the chance of being airborne when the sun disappeared. A search ensued for a suitable place to land away from those huge reptiles!

His northeasterly heading took him in the direction of Egypt. His sixth sense told him the Nile Valley may be populated, even though he knew for a fact it would be desolate in another 125 years. Nearing the Mediterranean Sea, he found an excellent place to land. The ship's speed decreased as the sun reached the horizon. The deficiency of ultraviolet rays forced Bill down. Quickly landing, he scouted the area for other signs of life. Certain he was alone, Bill made camp for the night. Dry firewood eluded Bill as the lush green trees thrived in the wet, humid conditions. Approximately a half mile from camp a small grove of trees lay lifelessly on the ground. Apparently they had been cut down by beavers or something. The branches were brittle enough to snap an adequate amount of smaller limbs off for a cozy fire. With the high density of humidity in the air, the fire created welcomed heat. Even though it was time to eat, Bill's appetite had been stifled by the events of the day. Too many unanswered questions ran rampant through his mind. Retrieving his log from the craft, Bill began recording everything that had transpired that day.

He finished his log by stating, "The strangest thing is, I know that 125 years from now this area will be an entirely different place. The water belt will be gone, the desert will be forming, and man will not exist in this area." The mere thought of man in the region prompted Bill to be prepared in the event he did encounter some people. His scientific brain kept telling him that man and dinosaurs did not exist at the same time, but he was beginning to doubt his original beliefs in science. While returning his log to the ship, he tried to locate the book on Egyptian hieroglyphics. Rummaging through the box, he discovered an unfamiliar white book zipped shut around the edges. Turning it over he found the Holy Bible with the name Michelle Hansen embossed in gold on the lower right-hand corner.

"She must have left it here the Sunday after church when I allowed the kids to play in the ship," Bill said as a smile warmed over his face. "Won't she be surprised when she finds out where it's been? I just hope I can get it back to her okay." Bill froze for a second as his smile faded, and he slowly wandered back to the fire sitting down. This was the first time he'd stopped to consider the ramifications of his situation and the possibilities of returning to his own time. The water belt eliminated any possible means of returning to his time. Consequently, Bill was trapped in the year 2351 B.C.

CHAPTER NINE

Bill was concentrating so intently on his dilemma, he momentarily blocked out the events surrounding him. The startling sound of something outside the camp brought him to his feet. Slowly backing up in the direction of the ship, he could hear movement in the bushes in front of him. Only a few steps from his ship the oncoming charge commenced from the bushes! Bill's original thought envisioned a lion or tiger eyeing him for a possible meal. Instead, to his amazement, an onrush of humans emerged from the brush! Bill dove head first into the Light Assimilator reaching for his .38 revolver under the seat. At the same moment, someone grabbed his left foot dragging him out of the craft! Barely reaching his gun at the last possible instant, he turned and fired it over the heads of his attackers. They jumped back five meters as Bill scanned the revolver at 20 native Egyptians. They were tall, large framed, light-skinned Caucasians dressed in robe-like clothing similar to his attire. After a momentary silence, the Egyptians began conversing among themselves. Bill's eyes widened recognizing their dialect as a variation of Hebrew. Although broken with a definite accent, Bill believed he might be able to communicate with them.

In Hebrew, Bill spoke very loud and slowly, "I AM FRIEND." They sprang back another five meters hearing their language spoken by this alien with the strange craft.

Finally, one brave soul stepped forward and announced, "WE ARE FRIEND TOO."

Bill smiled while cautiously lowering the gun. Rising from the ground, Bill extended his hand to the one who spoke to him. "My name is Bill."

The wary Egyptian stared at Bill's outstretched hand, then slowly raised his and said, "I am Kabe."

Bill grabbed his hand and shook it. Kabe's enormous hand equaled two of Bill's! "Let's sit down." Bill pointed towards the fire. Kabe nodded his head in agreement. Grabbing his Hebrew language book, he sat down around the fire with Kabe and his men. "Does everyone speak your language?" asked Bill doubtfully.

Looking puzzled Kabe replied, "Yes, everyone we know speaks the same tongue. We are surprised that you, too, speak our tongue. Where you hail from?"

"I come a long distance from the North and West," Bill replied. "Where did your people originate?"

"From the great paradise to the North and East. I am the ninth generation of our forefather Aban and Eva, his wife, who were created by our God, Re, in the paradise of Eben. His son, Rebe, came to this land after his brother Kone killed Alab." He paused for a moment while Bill was digesting the information. "Now, why are you and your vessel here?" Kabe asked demandingly. "Are you from the great night planet in the sky, or were you sent by Re's adversary Soden?"

Bill yearned to ask more questions. He could recollect some similarities between Kabe's story and something in the back of his mind from his early years, but now it was time for him to speak. The tone of Kabe's voice indicated a satisfying response was required. He didn't know what approach to take, but he had to start somewhere. "I come from the coastal land far to the west and years in the future."

At this response, Kabe shook his head no. "We do not understand years or future. We must take you to our king. He understands all."

"Who is this king and where is he located?" Bill asked.

"He is the great Pepi II (pronounced Phepi) located at Khufu. We leave at first light. No more questions tonight. We sleep now." Kabe was direct and powerfully in his orders.

Kabe demanded Bill's gun promising to deliver it personally to King Pepi II. Bill's initial reaction was to keep it, but that would have caused a confrontation, and Bill did not want to challenge him. His coaxing would not change Kabe's mind and only widen the gap between them. Luckily, Bill was successful in showing Kabe how to remove the exploding cartridges.

When Bill answered the question in terms they could not comprehend, he felt their feelings changed from one of friendliness to one of defensiveness. This new development troubled Bill. Kings in the olden days possessed great power and did not tolerate being intimidated by a foreigner. Escape, Bill felt, may be his best option, but he wasn't going anywhere without his ship. Deciding to survey the situation at first light, he bedded down for the night.

Morning came much too early for Bill. Rolling over he discovered two assigned men guarding his ship. "So much for the escape option," Bill muttered to himself. "Now I'll have to revert to plan B, whatever that is."

Rolling back over, he discovered Kabe staring at him. "Now we go," Kabe said decisively as he rose from his sleeping position.

"What about my vessel?" Bill asked stoutly.

"My men are strong. They will carry it." Motioning to his men, they immediately hoisted the craft up on their shoulders and headed to the south and east.

"I could fly you to King Pepi II," Bill said softly and slyly.

Kabe stopped in his tracks with an enraged stare penetrating Bill's person. No response was uttered, but for an instant, Bill feared for his safety. He could not understand why the suggestion of flying angered him so.

During the journey, Bill asked other questions of Kabe, but again he would not directly answer him. His only response remained that he must speak to Pepi II. The long journey gave Bill an ample amount of time to attempt to sort out these events. The names of Kabe's ancestors sounded strikingly similar to those used in old Bible stories.

That night around the fire, Bill retrieved Michelle's Bible researching the names Kabe mentioned in correlation to those in the scriptures.

Similarities included Adam and Eve in the Garden of Eden instead of Aban and Eva in the Paradise of Eben. Kone killing Alab mirrored Cain killing Abel, and Re's adversary Soden could have been Satan.

Bill continued glancing through the account of the creation when his mouth gaped open in astonishment. There before him was a verse capable of being the key to unlocking the earth's history and his dilemma! In Genesis 1:6-8 it read, "And God said, Let there be an expanse between the waters to separate water from water. So God made the expanse and separated the water under the expanse from the water above it. And it was so. God called the expanse SKY!"

Bill's amazement continued as he thought to himself, "Here in plain black and white modern man has an indication that a water belt existed around the earth and never gave it serious consideration because it was stated in the Bible! However, the majority of scientists agree this earth experienced the greenhouse effect worldwide at one time. The historian that composed the Bible knew it was up there and included it in his writings as another of God's creations."

Bill considered himself an atheist when it came to religion. Even though his ancestors were of the Jewish descent, he was not a follower of their beliefs. But anytime somebody wrote something concerning the earth's physical condition, he tended to believe it did exist. "Why would someone want to make up a story about a water belt existing above the sky if it never did?" He continued to look through Genesis to see if there were any other secrets to be revealed. He read where the great river running through the Garden of Eden consisted of four rivers: the Tigris, the Euphrates, the Pishon, and the Gihon. Checking his maps he could see where the first two still existed but not the latter two. "If I get the opportunity later, I'll have to look into this." He could not find where Adam had any sons named Rebe. All the scripture stated was that Adam had other sons and daughters. He did see where practically all generations down to Noah lived to be over 900 years old. And why not, with a belt of water filtering out the majority of the sun's damaging rays?

"Michael's findings were correct," Bill thought while shaking his head. "I should have listened to him. But of those who say they believe the Bible, few take it literally concerning the creation."

Reading on, Bill discovered that a short time after the Great Flood, construction of the Tower of Babel began. God confused the people's languages so they would scatter and populate the earth. The location of this tower matched the area of the massive ziggurat he'd seen on his last stop in 2225 B.C. "If there is any truth to this Tower of Babel story, it would explain why these people speak Hebrew. Maybe only one language exists on the earth at this time," Bill reasoned even though he had serious doubts about its validity.

He prepared to stop for the night as he came to the "who begot who" section. As he glanced down the page, something caught his eye. Here it said, again in plain black and white, that a man was given the name Peleg because that was the time the land divided! His incoming flight revealed the land masses of the earth together only separated by rivers and valleys. This historical writing described the early earth history exactly as it existed, and modern man would not believe or even consider it because these facts were intermingled with writings about an all-powerful God.

During this time Kabe patiently sat, intently watching Bill reading this strange material. Casually walking over behind him, Kabe looked over Bill's shoulder trying to determine what this hand-held object with small markings on it could be. Bill jotted the pertinent information in his log concerning the findings he had discovered.

Kabe's curiosity could not be contained any longer. "What is purpose of these items, and why do you make markings on one of them?"

Bill sternly glared up at Kabe. "I will not answer your questions until you answer mine."

A hush spread over the camp as Kabe harshly returned the stare at his captive. Bill began to wish he had not quipped such a quick response.

Finally, Kabe replied, "What is your question?"

With a sigh of relief Bill asked, "How long before we get to Khufu, and I am allowed to see your king?"

"One full arch of the sun," Kabe quickly replied. "Now," he demanded grabbing Bill's books, "What are purpose of these?"

Bill began, "I come from many arches of the sun after today. This book, called the Bible, has many events stored in it. I can look at these markings, and they tell me the story of what occurred. In the other book, I record a history of my travels. By my symbols others can learn from my experiences. These writings are very similar to your hieroglyphics."

This response pleased Kabe as he sat down next to Bill. Late into the night Bill attempted to answer all of his questions. By the time they had finished, Bill felt assured he had won back Kabe's trust and friendship, and Bill knew a friend would be needed when he reached the king.

Bill needed more knowledge pertaining to the king, so he asked Kabe if he could look up some information in the Light Assimilator. Kabe trusted his new friend, but watched very intently as Bill began punching up information on his computer. Bill wanted as many details as he could get about King Pepi II.

He was able to read about the king's long reign and the great number of wives and children he had. He discovered Pepi liked to travel, and that detail could give Bill an advantage. Finally, it talked about how King Pepi II was the last ruler of the Old Kingdom of Egypt. Following his reign, Egypt mysteriously went silent until many years later. Historians feel this decline could have been climate change related. Bill could only smile as he turned off the computer. "Climate change would be an understatement," Bill commented as the climbed back out of his ship.

CHAPTER TEN

At first light, the band of men broke camp continuing their trudging journey to Khufu. Bill's legs and feet ached from the previous day's activities. By midmorning, he could barely keep up with the eight men carrying his craft, not to mention the rest of the group. Their strength and endurance amazed Bill as they steadily traversed the flat, green countryside. Bill knew he must reach their destination as quickly as possible and fought to keep up the pace. Kabe had mentioned the city stretched along the Great River, which Bill assumed was the Nile.

The high humidity soaked Bill's clothing and made breathing difficult. Now he could understand why plant life flourished under these conditions. Since the sun's rays could not evaporate water into the atmosphere, it was extremely possible that it never rained, but it didn't need to under these circumstances. What water did evaporate saturated the air and everything on the earth. When asked, Kabe did not understand water falling from the sky, so Bill assumed his presumption was correct.

From the air, Bill had observed thousands of dinosaurs, but on the ground their presence had not been noted. Inquiring of Kabe, Bill asked, "Where are all the great monsters of the forest?"

"Behemoth like the forest, but do not like man. Though they are big, they are not smart. We inhabited areas that did not have many trees. Many trees we cut down. Behemoth does not want to approach our living areas."

"Where do your people live?" Bill asked.

"The majority of our tribes live close to the Great River. Some people live next to the Endless Waters. The outcasts are sent to the forest to live with Behemoth because they do not fit in with our people."

"Why don't some people fit in?" Bill inquired.

"If their mind or body is not right, they are sent away. We do not want those types in our midst. They will breed more like them," Kabe stated authoritatively totally believing in that system.

Bill stopped short of arguing this point, even though he did not agree with it. Many civilizations around the world had attempted these tactics with the last being Hitler. Each time resulted in rebellion and decay. This system helped explain why all of Kabe's men were so big and strong. They may be the result of selective breeding. This feature combined with the ideal living conditions surrounding them helped the human and animal species to develop.

"How old are you, Kabe?" Bill asked.

Shaking his head, Kabe stated, "I do not know. Age and time are not my concern, only the King's. I do know my children have had children seven times."

Bill interpreted this to mean there were eight generations of Kabes running around. Under these conditions, human development would be slow. Assuming man did not reproduce until age 30 would give Kabe an attained age of approximately 250 years old while he only looked to be 45!

By noon, the pinnacles of the pyramids gleamed in the distance. Late that afternoon the city appeared on the horizon. Khufu's proximity matched that of modern day Cairo spreading out on both sides of the Nile. Bill marveled at the city's infrastructure. He was amazed at its modern construction. The dried brick buildings hauntingly resembled those of Jerusalem in 60 A.D. It seemed odd that man's technological advances in the next 3000 years would not considerably change. But since 1900 A.D. to Bill's era, knowledge had skyrocketed.

People began emerging from the city to observe this strange contraption being carried by Kabe's men. Bill requested that his ship were left outside of the city so it would be less apt to be damaged by vandals. Kabe agreed and ordered two of his men to guard the ship.

Little did Kabe know of Bill's ulterior motive. In the event of a quick get-a-way, Bill wanted his ship in an unconfined location. Bill grabbed a few odds and ends out of the Light Assimilator to help win the king's favor. He also took his log and reading material to help pass the time.

Inside, the bustle of the city reminded Bill of Jerusalem. Women carried vases of water to their homes; vendors sold their wares in the open market, while little children ran and played in the narrow streets. Bill felt like a midget amongst these giants. Even the majority of the women dwarfed Bill's stature. Kabe led him toward a large stone structure set apart from the other buildings in the area. Could this structure be the king's palace, Bill wondered as he asked, "What is this place?"

"This is temple to the Sun God, Re," Kabe stated proudly. "You will stay here while I go confer with the great Pepi II."

"Where is the king?" Bill questioned as he saw Kabe leaving the premises. He was afraid of being left there for days waiting for the king's good pleasure to see him.

"He is across the Great River in the Temple of the King," he replied pointing to the top of a structure adjacent the opposite bank of the Nile. "I will go there now and bring back word soon."

"Thank you. Your speed is appreciated," Bill complimented.

Half of Kabe's men remained at the Temple with the order to provide for Bill's needs as long as he didn't leave the building. "So much for a chance to return to my ship out the front door," Bill said to himself as he glanced around the inside of the Temple. "Maybe I can sneak around and find the back door."

The curator of the building seemed curious as to Bill's presence and guarded nature. The man's inquisitiveness gave Bill the opportunity to ask a few questions and possibly locate another way out. "What are your duties here?"

"If you do not already know, I am the Head Priest of the Sun God, Re," he proudly responded.

Remembering his history, Bill recalled the Egyptian God of later times was called Ra (pronounced Rah). A question immediately arose in Bill's mind how a variance in the Egyptian God's name could occur. "And what is the purpose of this god, Re?"

The priest looked shocked. He knew that any citizen of the region would know the answer to that question. "Where do you hail from?" demanded the priest.

"I will tell you," promised Bill, "if you answer my questions." He hoped to flood the priest with an overwhelming number of queries and eventually discover a secondary way out.

The priest consented and began, "The God Re (pronounced Ray) is the Sun God. He is the most powerful of all gods. Without him, we could not see and our crops would not grow."

Bill was impressed by the fact these people realized it took the sun to make plants grow. "How do you know that plants need sunshine?"

"Simple," the priest responded. "If you leave a plant in a dark room, it will wither and die. If you place it close to a window, it will bend in the direction of the light."

"How do you appease your god?" Bill quickly continued not giving the priest a chance to change the subject.

"The day when the sun is in the sky the longest we choose one pure maiden to go to Re. Being chosen is a great honor for her and her family. A group of women whom man has not known will draw lots. The chosen one will be taken to the top of the tower and stay there until he has joined her spirit. Her sacrifice guarantees us good crops and prosperity, and is a proper atonement for all the people of the land."

This type of belief did not surprise Bill. Most ancient cultures believed in human sacrifice to appease their gods. Bill could see the tower in the courtyard where the young maiden would be led to the top and probably strapped down to die of thirst and exposure.

Bill hesitated momentarily as he gazed out the opening at the tower. His hesitation gave the priest an opportunity to ask, "Now, where are you from?"

Forced to respond, Bill thought he'd have a little fun with the priest'. "I come from the Northwest corner of the earth. I have traveled a long distance to explore your country. We have great magic in my land." Stating that, he pulled a lighter out of his robe and flicked his Bic. "Now lead me to the exit at the rear of the temple or you will die!"

The priest stunned and amazed at this wonder backed up fearful of Bill's power. Bill slowly walked towards him with the flame rising into the air. The priest, keeping a close eye on the fire, backed into a stone bench falling seat first to the floor. Startled, he scurried to his feet and darted into an adjacent room. Bill smiled and chuckled to himself as he began to follow the priest.

Before he could reach the doorway, he was surrounded by Kabe's troops. At that moment, the door swung open with Kabe and the remainder of his men behind him. "The king will see you at first light. You will spend the night in the Waiting Chamber of the King's Temple. We go now."

A raft-like vessel guided by strands of twisted fiber provided the means for crossing the river. Bill's questions concerning the king fell on deaf ears as Kabe kept repeating, "Only the king can answer your questions." Apparently the king had instructed Kabe not to talk to him, which greatly disturbed Bill. Up till now, Kabe remained the only ally he had, but this development left Bill alone in a strange land at a strange time. So many questions concerning history had been solved and so many more were waiting to be answered. But first he had to find a way out of this predicament.

The King's Temple dwarfed the surrounding buildings. The large stone structure rose three stories majestically eclipsing any other buildings in both beauty and grandeur. Kabe's men remained at the front gate while he led Bill into the palace and down a long dark hallway to a huge wooden door. Removing the beam across the door, Kabe motioned for Bill to enter.

Swinging the door open, Bill beheld his lowly accommodations for the night. The 12' x 12' room contained what could be construed as a table and chair, and a lumpy looking pad in the corner Bill assumed was his bed. Three long vertical windows 6" wide in the west wall provided some lighting for the otherwise dingy room. "No chance for escape through them," Bill thought to himself as Kabe announced he would be bringing food soon. He promptly shut the door leaving Bill alone in his new home.

Dust covered everything. Bill circled the room taking a mental inventory of his surroundings. Sitting at the bench-like table, he brought his log up to date. Originally, Bill had looked forward to meeting a real king, but now an uneasy feeling crept over him. In this day and age, kings execute people for looking the wrong direction. One wrong step could prove fatal.

The sound of the door turned Bill's head. Kabe entered the room with a large tray heaping with edibles. "Do you eat this much at every meal?" Bill asked staring at the plate.

"You look like your small body needed some nourishment." Bill glanced up to see a smile forming on Kabe's face. It quickly faded as Kabe sternly said, "No more talk now. I take you to King Pepi II at first light. A guard will be outside your door if you need help."

Bill wanted to ask what he was eating, but Kabe turned and exited the room. "Probably just as well. It would only spoil my appetite if I knew I was feasting on a lizard or something comparable." The meal consisted of a flat pancake-like bread with an indistinguishable flavor. Numerous strips of some form of dried jerky filled the remainder of the tray. A cup of green sauce sat next to the plate, but he wasn't going to take any chances with that! A large brown flask of water provided the liquids for the meal.

Afterward, he sat down in his guarded room attempting to sort out his options. He had devised a plan to deal with the king, so that did not immediately concern him. Bill's thoughts turned to his entrapment in this era.

The presence of the water belt forced his ship out of light speed. During his earlier deviations from light speed, it took 11 days for his ship to coast back to earth time. If the coasting factor remained constant, then approximately ten days from the time he landed, the water belt should not exist. The next question is what's going to happen to that ball of water surrounding the earth? Bill recalled the violent shaking occurring the few seconds before being forced to sub-light speed. "Could it be the entire belt falls to the earth?" Bill wondered rising to his feet and paced the floor trying to find the answer. "At light speed, those few seconds of shaking translate into a couple months on earth. But if the whole belt fell to the planet's surface, it would only take a matter of minutes and I would have been knocked from the sky."

Bill searched his brain-for the solution. Recalling his most recent stop in time he remembered the retreating ice cap visible from the Great Lakes region. Michael's theory popped into his mind like a light bursting forth its essence! With his finger pointing in the air, Bill's face lit up as he excitedly exclaimed, "The comet is coming!"

He hypnotically stared into nothingness as he theorized, "Ice particles from the tail of the comet will break through the water belt clamping down on the magnetic poles of the earth. The drastic change in temperature will condense the remainder of the belt and rain torrents on the earth for weeks! The earth will be thrown into an oblong orbit while rotating on its new axis. The water from above will raise the ocean levels to their modern day depths. Animals in the northern and southern regions will be quick frozen. Depending on the quantity of water up there, the majority of man and animals could perish from this catastrophe." Pounding his fist on the table Bill resounded, "And if I don't get myself back in the air, I could be one of those perishing!"

A dreadful shiver descended down Bill's spine at the mere thought of drowning. He wanted to continue his theory on the coming events, but the light of day vanished into darkness, and he had to prepare himself for his confrontation with the king. As he sat down on the bed for the night, one sobering fact came to mind. It wouldn't matter how much he discovered about the past if he didn't get back home to share his findings.

"This is my third full day since my ship fell from light speed. That gives me up to seven days to resolve this problem." The "up to" part bothered him. He assumed, due to the partial water belt being present during the shaking, his ship may have coasted to a stop quicker. "Unfortunately, I don't know how many days I have left until the tail of the comet changes the complexion of this world forever," Bill said despairingly as he reclined back on his mattress for the night. Bill tossed and turned for hours with everything rolling through his mind. He couldn't complain about his sleeping arrangements. The straw mattress wrapped in leather felt much better than the hard ground he had endured the past couple nights. It was midnight before he drifted off to sleep.

CHAPTER ELEVEN

The startling sound of vigorous pounding on his door jolted Bill from a deep sleep. He rolled over beholding the light of a new day beaming through the narrow windows as Kabe burst into the room, "It is time for you to meet the king."

In the process of getting ready Bill asked, "When are you allowed to return home?"

"I am free to leave when I deliver you to King Pepi II," he replied factually not even glancing at Bill as he spoke.

Bill could sense Kabe's unwillingness to talk due to the apparent orders from the king. In an attempt to leave on a friendly note, Bill said, "In that case, I may not see you again. I would like to thank you for not harming me when you and your men discovered my presence. It would have been very easy for you to have killed me and not bothered bringing me here. You have provided me with food and answered my questions. As a token of our friendship, I would like to give you a firestick."

Bill held out one of his lighters with the flame rising high. He showed Kabe how to light it, and after a few attempts Kabe managed to light the flame. This accomplishment brought a welcomed smile from his native companion. Bill firmly shook Kabe's hand and looking at him directly in the eyes said, "Friend."

Kabe led the way as they walked down another long dark hallway. At the end, a stone archway led into an open courtyard. In the center of the courtyard appeared a man seated on an elevated throne. Two guards shadowed the back side of the throne. Immediately Kabe knelt on one knee and pulled Bill down with him. "Do not gaze at him,"

Bill heard Kabe whisper as they knelt. With their heads lowered they patiently waited.

"Rise." Slowly they rose to their feet continuing to stare at the floor. "Come forward before the great king," commanded the man authoritatively. Kabe pushed Bill towards the throne while Kabe slowly retreated from the courtyard. Bill was now alone with the most powerful man in the land. Raising his head to face the king, he beheld a big man, similar to the others he had observed, standing tall with powerful shoulders and legs. Bill held out his hand to greet the king, but there was no response.

"Kneel at the feet of the great Pepi II."

Submissively obeying, Bill returned to this lowly position. He wanted the king to be assured this stranger yielded no threat to his preeminent power and authority. By taking this humble approach, the king was not apt to be. on the defensive and more likely to respond on a friendly basis, Bill hoped.

After what seemed to be an eternity of silence the king spoke, "Kabe tells me you are from another land, possibly another time. Is this correct?"

Bill looked up and responded cautiously, "Yes it is, great King. Your man Kabe is a fair and honest man. He should be commended for a job well done." Bill wanted to get a chance to praise Kabe before commencing his story.

"I come from a land a long distance from here, but it is also many seasons from now. My people send you gifts of their time." Out of his robe Bill drew a note pad and a ball point pen demonstrating them to the king.

"Kabe has told me about such petty things," the king replied sternly. "He also mentioned you have in your possession a firestick to make fire." Bill revealed a lighter and demonstrated it for him. "Kabe told me it was the magic of your time, but I do not believe in magic. How does this firestick work?" demanded the king.

Obviously the king's intelligence dwarfed the majority of this era's inhabitants. Bill proceeded to inform him how a little spark created within the lighter ignites the liquid fuel. The king inspected the lighter momentarily and said, "So when all the liquid is used up there will be no more fire. Where do I find more of this liquid? I must have it to light fires all over the city!"

The king's initial comprehension of the lighter amazed Bill. The king was not going to be as easy to impress as he first hoped. Bill tried to explain to the king how the liquid was only found deep under the ground in certain parts of the world. He didn't bother to mention there would have to be a mass slaughter of dinosaurs before fossil fuels would even exist.

The king, not getting a feasible answer, moved on to another subject. "Kabe told me you possess a weapon of great power. I would like to see a demonstration of this weapon. Kabe brought it to me with a grave warning not to grip it or insert these tiny metal sticks."

Bill had hoped the subject of the gun would not be brought up. He knew if the king felt threatened, he would have Bill incarcerated forever. On the other hand, the gun may be the only thing in his possession that may impress the king. Bill safely retrieved the revolver from the king's table, checked the chamber, and handed the gun to the king. It didn't' take long for the king to discover pulling the trigger induced a response from the device. He intently watched the cylinder rotate as the hammer went click on the firing pin. "Do the small metal sticks go inside of here?" inquired the king.

"Yes. These are bullets," Bill said holding up one of the cartridges. "They are projected from the gun and are capable of penetrating something a long distance away. May I demonstrate it for you?"

The king hesitated, and then handed the gun back to Bill. Loading one shell in the chamber Bill scanned the courtyard for something to shoot. Approximately ten meters away a large bowl of fruit graced a wooden pedestal. "May I destroy your bowl?" The king nodded in approval and Bill prepared to fire. Marksmanship was not one of Bill's strong suits. Slowly and carefully he took aim. As Bill squeezed the trigger, a thunderous explosion echoed through the courtyard. Bill's low shot ricocheted off the table throwing the bowl up into the air and scattered the fruit.

Immediately the king's aides rushed forward. The king, not feeling threatened, motioned for them to retreat. Examining the bowl, the king carefully observed the forceful results of the shot. Walking back to his throne, he gestured for Bill to come forward and sit in the chair next to him. Examining the revolver, the king sniffed the smoke corning from the end of the barrel. "Is there fire in the gun?"

Bill tried to explain how a great burst of fire is contained in each bullet. "The explosion of fire projects the bullet to what you are pointing at."

"I must try this thing called gun," the king insisted. What choice did Bill have? Reassembling the bowl of fruit he loaded one shell in the revolver. He positioned the king five meters from the bowl to give him a better opportunity. Bill moved behind the king and helped hold his arms steady while locking his elbows. Once set, he instructed the king to pull back the trigger slowly. The startling jolt of the discharging gun knocked the king backward sending both of them to the ground! By some miracle the king managed to hit the bowl as fruit littered the paved floor. The king, sprawled out on the ground with his eyes a mile wide! He started chuckling. Then all out laughter erupted! When he calmed down, his silent gaze looked back at Bill. "You are from another time, aren't you?" Bill nodded his head yes as he assisted the king back to his throne. "What do you want from us?" inquired the king seriously.

Bill felt that now he had won the king's favor. "I do not want anything from you, great king. I am trapped in your time because of the water belt surrounding the earth. Not long from now it will disappear, and I will be able to travel back to my time."

"Then the old man was right," the king responded to himself.

"What?" Bill questioned curiously. "What old man? Does someone else know the water belt is going to fall? Does he know exactly when? Can I talk to this person?" Bill rattled off the questions so fast he didn't give the king a chance to respond.

Eagerly Bill looked on as the king replied, "Not many seasons ago, an old man from the north came and announced his God was going to destroy this world if man did not turn from his wicked ways. The waters from the heavens would fall and cover the earth, but he did not say exactly when it would happen. I do not believe in gods, so I sent him away. I don't even remember what his name was. Now my astrologers tell me a great star is coming this way, and something traumatic could occur soon. Then you show up informing me of such matters. Please tell me what is going to happen?"

"I do not know exactly what will occur, but I do know the great star is called a comet. It will come very close to the earth and fall on the extreme northern and southern parts of this planet. That will cause the water belt to fall from the heavens. This event will befall on the entire earth in a few more arches of the sun. You and your people should be prepared to escape to the highest mountain possible."

Silence filled the courtyard as the king contemplated the significance of this revelation. Suddenly the king resonantly clapped his hands three times. His personal aid entered through a doorway and approached the throne, "Bring food for me and my guest." Bill perceived that the king wanted to drop the subject concerning the water belt since there was nothing he could do to change it.

While they ate, the topic changed to the events of Bill's world. The next couple hours Bill tried to explain how modern man harnessed the power in the liquid that lit the firestick and the power that fired the bullet. Bill went on to tell how these great powers had been utilized in machines, manufacturing materials, self-powered vehicles, and even into planes that soared into the sky like an eagle.

At that point the king broke in, "I'd give my firstborn to be able to fly."

Leaning back in his chair Bill shrewdly smiled. "I can make you fly like an eagle, and the only thing it will cost you is the answer to a few questions and my freedom."

The king contemplated the situation for a minute. "If you can actually make me fly above the city so my people can see me, I will grant your wishes."

This development appeared to be the break Bill had been waiting for. He stuck his hand out and grabbed the king's to consummate the agreement. Bill smiled, slapped the king on the back, and enthusiastically said, "Let's go soar like an eagle!"

CHAPTER TWELVE

The king summoned ten of his men to accompany them, traveling across the river to the Light Assimilator. Kabe's men faithfully continued to guard the craft, but Kabe was nowhere to be seen. The king released the men from their duty and informed them they were free to return to their homes and families.

The structure of the ship intrigued the king. He wanted to know everything about the craft and how it operated. Bill had a difficult time trying to explain ultraviolet rays and what powered the ship. When satisfied with Bill's explanations, the king decided to give this contraption a test flight. By now a vast crowd from the city gathered around the craft. Anytime the king went anywhere, the people followed out of curiosity. This time they would not be disappointed.

Bill unloaded half of his supplies allowing ample space for his passenger. When the king's aide discovered his sovereign planned on getting in this odd device with this stranger, he became extremely concerned with the eminent danger or the possibility of his king being hijacked. The king reassured the aide that Bill was his friend and not to worry.

After the guards turned the craft in a westerly direction, the two men climbed into the cockpit and prepared for takeoff. Bill knew this action was something he had vowed never to do. During the past two days, he had revealed himself and his invention to people in the distant past. By doing this, he assumed the responsibility of changing the course of history forever. At this point in time, Bill felt it really didn't matter. Odds were against any of these individuals being alive a week from now.

Bill's chances of survival and returning home hinged on his ability to impress the king.

The people cheered as the craft accelerated down the path picking up more and more speed until the wheels lifted off the ground. The king dug his fingernails in Bill's headrest holding on for dear life. Once in the air, Bill slowly circled the people they had left on the ground.

"Wave to your subjects," Bill said. "Show them how brave their king is."

At this suggestion, the king took a deep breath and let go of his penetrating death grip on Bill's seat. Glancing out the window he quickly latched on to Bill's chair again. Finally, after a couple loops around the anxious crowd, the king looked out the window mustering up the courage to wave to his people. A roar rose from the crowd as they witnessed their leader's bravery.

This new found confidence prompted the king's command, "Now, let me see my city."

"Yes sir," Bill cheerfully replied turning toward Khufu and commenced circling the city. The people of the city ran from their homes pointing to the sky while others ran down the street announcing the news. Some of the inhabitants reacted hysterically until they realized their king was safe. The people stood in a state of amazement watching their king soar above the city in this shiny bird. The king, now at the height of his glory, had transformed himself into a god.

Bill could see it now. Someday archeologists would discover ancient paintings of two men flying in a craft over the city. "That should keep the researchers scratching their heads!"

Since they were airborne, Bill suggested swinging over and taking a look at the pyramids. The three pyramids of Giza rose grandly before them. Their fully polished limestone casings mirrored the afternoon sun completely intact from top to bottom. Bill began asking questions regarding their construction, but the king stopped him and said he would answer all his questions later. Right now, the king wanted to enjoy this wonderful experience. The Sphinx lay ahead guarding the tombs of the kings and pharaohs. The Sphinx's completely exposed body towered above the landscape. Bill recalled his last stop in time when only the Sphinx's head protruded from the pebbly sand. "It must be the coming onrush of water that will conceal it with sand. That would explain why the sand resembled that of ocean sand rather than wind-blown desert sand!"

The two of them spent the rest of the afternoon flying around Pepi's kingdom. Their flight took them to the Endless Waters, which was the Mediterranean Sea. And over the Red Sea, which wasn't much more than a river due to the low water levels in the oceans. As the sun descended toward the horizon, Bill insisted they must return.

News had spread throughout the city of the king's adventure. A crowd ten times the size of the one that witnessed their departure presented themselves to see their fearless leader land. Many in the throng knelt down and bowed their heads as the ship touched down, and the king emerged with his hands raised high. The crowd yelled and chanted parading behind them the entire way back to the king's temple. Bill had inadvertently made King Pepi II the most powerful and godlike king that ever ruled, and the king knew it.

Immediately following the evening meal, the king announced he was going to retire. "What about my questions?" Bill inquired somewhat disgusted.

"I will answer all your questions tomorrow," stated the king and he walked out of the room leaving Bill questioning the king's intentions.

While being escorted back to his quarters, they passed a large window. Bill stopped for a moment gazing at the night sky. There, in the distance, far beyond the water belt it appeared, the first comet Bill had ever seen! The dud of Halley's Comet back in 1986 hadn't impressed anyone, but Bill could tell this would be no dud. The comet's trajectory produced a massive tail pointing straight up. The ice particles fleeing the enormous snowball chose a repulsive tract from the sun's rays giving a false indication of its actual directional path. Bill was no astrologer, but it looked like he may have at least a couple days before the comet would confront the earth and its inhabitants.

CHAPTER THIRTEEN

Early the next morning Bill prepared to meet the king and ask his questions. He was also prepared to depart from this area. The sooner he could leave these people and the ever present thought of captivity, the sooner he might be able to calculate a plan for his survival. Minutes turned into hours as Bill anxiously awaited the king's aide to arrive and accompany him to the king. As the hours passed, Bill's anticipation turned to uneasiness as he began to wonder if the king changed his mind. Finally, around mid-morning, the door swung open. Much to Bill's surprise stood King Pepi II!

"Now, what questions do you have for the great king?" he asked confidently sitting down in the chair next to Bill.

Bill, not wanting to inquire why the king came to him, went ahead with his questions. "First of all, I would like the detailed information on the building of the great pyramids. Why they were constructed, how they were built, how long did it take, and how many men did it take?" Bill poised with pen in hand over his notebook ready for every word the king would say.

"Why do we build the great pyramids?" the king reiterated. "Very simple. Only one out of every four people farms the land for their existence. Some people are builders or merchants. Unfortunately, many people of our land do not have a trade. They looked to the great pharaohs to provide food for them and their families. The government has ample amounts of food to give these people, but it was our decision that they must work for their food. The pyramids and other great works of this land provide a way to employ these people. If a man will work 100

us to achieve a perfectly level base. The surrounding hills of the area provide ample amounts of sandstone. This softer rock is easily hewn and constitutes the main stone used in the construction of the pyramids. We initially use copper chisels and hammers to cut the stone. We then insert a series of wooden wedges soaking them with water after they are securely embedded into the crevices. The wedges expand cracking the rock along the grooved lines the stonecutters have made. The stones align together on the pyramid in the same order they are extracted from the hillside. This procedure enables us to fit them tightly together strengthening the structure."

"One of the things I want to know," Bill interrupted, "is how did you get the stones from the hillside to the construction site and then up the pyramid? Each of those stones must weigh a couple tons!"

The king sat back in his chair, looked at Bill and replied, "I can see if all your people are small and weak like you, it would be hard to understand. I do not comprehend your word tons, but each stone is cut so eight men can handle it. The cut stone is placed on a sled and transported to the site. The workmen construct a ramp of sand ascending around the pyramid. Upon completion, the ramp is dismantled as the limestone cap is glazed over the sandstone from the top down. Transporting the granite rock used inside the tomb created the most difficulties. Many days up the Great River is the home of the mountain supplying this extremely heavy rock. The men load each stone on a raft and float them down the river. The loading and unloading from the raft at first caused some problems. After much trial and error, our foremen devised a water counterbalance hoisting the stone from the land, swinging it over the raft, slowly releasing the water from the counterbalance, and lowering the stone on the raft. The same procedure removes the granite at the other end."

"And you did all this just to build a tomb for your kings and pharaohs?" Bill cut in.

"We had to do something to employ our people," the king rebutted, "and some of the previous leaders were egotistical enough. to demand something built in recognition of them."

"People are still like that in my world," Bill agreed nodding his head. "Speaking of people, what do your subjects do in their spare time?"

"These people are not very intelligent. They do not comprehend numbers or time. Many are hard workers and enjoy doing physical things. They are loyal followers to the king's command and to the commands of Re. They fear the power of Re. I relay all messages from Re, but as you probably know, Re does not exist. He is an excellent tool for the king to use as leverage so the people do not revolt."

"Why don't you quit the human sacrifices to Re if he doesn't exist?" Bill asked hoping the king would reconsider that practice.

"You do not see," replied the king. "We sacrifice to Re to keep fear instilled in their hearts. If anything in the kingdom ever does go wrong, I tell the people Re is angry with them, and they must pay a pittance to him. Naturally, all payments come to the palace."

The king continued, "I arrived late this morning because I spoke to my people earlier. They were very impressed by my flight around the kingdom. Did you know you were sent by Re and are his personal messenger to me?"

Bill could smell a rat as the king smiled and clapped his hands twice signaling his aide to enter the room. The king pointed at Bill, and his assistant immediately grabbed Bill by the arms. The king searched the room confiscating Bill's lighter. Pulling the revolver from his robe, he raised them triumphantly into the air. "For that reason you are going to remain here until this comet in the sky passes. The people believe you have been sent to protect us. Your presence will instill peace until whatever happens. If you try to escape, you will be executed. In that event, I will tell the people you were sent by Soden masquerading as a messenger of Re. To kill a messenger of Soden would make me more powerful than any king or pharaoh before me!"

The king's smile exhibited a sense of pride and ingenuity as he strutted out of the room. He ordered his aide not to allow anyone to visit Bill or for any reason let him leave.

Speechless and stunned Bill watched the heavy wooden door slam in front of him. His worst nightmare began to unfold. His hypothesis of the near future told him he had to leave soon. He also had no doubt the king would execute him if he was caught trying to escape, but what choice did he have? When the comet did strike its death blow to the water belt, the low-lying regions adjacent to the Nile River would inevitably be flooded, and he would perish anyway. The only real chance of survival was the choice he didn't want, escape.

First, he surveyed the room to check out his possibilities. Only one wall had windows, but they were very close to the ceiling and much too small for him to possibly fit through. Only one door in the room provided an exit, and he knew all too well whose presence was there to greet him on the other side. Just to make sure, Bill thought he would peek out the door to investigate. A firm resistance told Bill it was locked. The long wooden brace placed across the door securely held it from the outside.

"Now what can I do?" Bill pondered as he plopped down in the chair. The late afternoon sun shone through the narrow windows as Bill placed his elbows on the table, interlocking his fingers, and rested his chin on his thumbs while staring at the huge wooden door. Action must be taken soon. It wouldn't do any good to return to his ship if there weren't enough light to power his escape. Old T.V. reruns raced through Bill's mind as he tried to visualize a good escape plan.

"If they proceed according to schedule, they should bring me one more meal today. That might be my only chance to get out," Bill said as he rose up from his chair and began pacing the room. Suddenly he stopped, and his eyes lit up as a scene from one of his favorite shows came to mind. Bill ran over to the door and yelled, "How long until I can eat? I'm starved."

The aide replied, "I will see that it gets here soon."

Bill scurried around the room looking for what he needed. Within minutes, the muffled sound of the brace being removed froze Bill in his tracks. The door creaked open, and the king's aide appeared carrying Bill's dinner tray. He cautiously stopped a few steps into the room.

"Where has that little guy gone?" the aide thought as he scanned the room. His eyes stopped when he noticed a curtain made out of the bed blanket hanging on the wall. Under the bottom edge of the curtain peeked the rounded front of a pair of sandals. Setting the tray down, he quietly snuck over to the curtain. Doubling up his large fist, he struck a mighty blow to the area where Bill's midsection should be. With great pain, the aide contacted nothing but stone wall! At that moment, the curtain ripped open from the other side revealing the bare-footed trickster. Holding two large handfuls of dust, Bill thrust them into the unsuspecting man's eyes. Bill pushed the temporarily blinded aide to the floor, threw the blanket over him and dashed out of the room. He quickly pushed the door shut and started to insert the heavy brace when two strong hands grabbed him by the shoulders!

"Where do you think you're going?" boomed a deep voice Bill had not previously heard.

Very shortly, the aide stumbled through the doorway still rubbing his eyes. "Oh, I see you met our cook!" he exclaimed with a big smile on his face. "He always waits around so he can get his dishes back." The cook firmly held Bill by the shoulders from the backside as the aide said, "I think I owe you this." With that, he delivered a powerful blow to Bill's stomach doubling him over. Gasping for air, Bill dropped to his knees wilting face first onto the floor.

The aide's strong arms snatched Bill off the floor throwing him back into the room saying, "I think the king will be very glad to hear you tried to escape. I would kill you myself, but I will have more fun watching him torture you!"

Distraught, the door slammed behind Bill, leaving him alone in a state of confusion. He thought he had covered all the bases of his plan. "It always worked on T.V.," he said dejectedly. Now he had to deal with the realism that there may be no more chances to escape. And that he may indeed die when the morning came. Having lost all hope, Bill mournfully crawled in bed and bitterly wept remembering his life and friends back home.

CHAPTER FOURTEEN

A disturbance outside Bill's door in the wee hours of the morning aroused him from a restless sleep. He sat up in bed hearing the heavy beam dislodged from the brace. As the door creaked open, Bill knew the time had come for him to face the king and possibly endure the final moments of his life. Through the darkness Bill heard the familiar voice, "Friend, it is I, Kabe. We must go quickly."

Bill sprang from his bed leaping into Kabe's outstretched arms giving him a big hug. "Thank you my friend," Bill expressed appreciatively. "How did you know I needed help?"

"Talk later. We go now." Kabe responded. He had gagged and tied the king's aide. Kabe dragged him into the room while Bill gathered his books and belongings. They braced the door behind them heading down the dreadfully dark corridor out of the palace. Bill now realized he could not have completed this journey on his own. Exiting the palace, Kabe turned left following the shadows of the structure. Kabe knew all the back alleys traveling through the city undetected. He also had arranged for a boat to transport them across the river. During the crossing, Kabe explained how he had listened to the speech the king presented to the people. After hearing the speech, Kabe knew Bill's life was in imminent danger.

"I felt in the dead of night would be best time to attempt a breakout," Kabe reckoned. "I could not endanger the lives of my men, so I came alone."

"But what about you?" Bill inquired insistently. "Aren't you endangering yourself?"

"It doesn't matter," Kabe reasoned. "You are my friend. What the king is planning is wrong. I will go to land far away where King Pepi II will not find me."

The sun's beaming essence peeked over the eastern horizon as the two neared the edge of the city. Bill and Kabe cautiously peered around the last house on the edge of town. The two guards left by King Pepi II replacing Kabe's men continued their vigilant watch of the vessel, but at least the ship looked to be in the same condition as he had left it.

"Do you have your weapon called gun?" Kabe whispered.

"No. The king seized it," was Bill's dismal response.

"But the guards don't know that," Kabe replied cunningly. Take my firestick and pretend you will hurt me if they do not leave the ship. I will convince them."

Impressed by Kabe's ingenuity, Bill reached up and put his left arm around Kabe's neck while pointing the lighter at his head. They slowly walked out into the open toward the Light Assimilator.

The guards began advancing towards them when Kabe yelled, "He has great firestick! It can kill a man at 50 steps! Leave the ship and he will spare us all."

One of the guards responded, "The king will kill us also if we desert our post. Surely he cannot stop all three of us."

Kabe enhanced his story. "He has already killed the king and his aide. Since the king is dead, you will not be held responsible for anything. You have already witnessed his great power and magic. I suggest you do not test him."

All this time Bill remained silent. The guards glanced at each other and shook their heads no. "We cannot disobey our orders," one stated.

Kabe whispered back at Bill, "Kill me!"

Bill erupted with a thunderous arcing noise. Kabe grabbed his head while gyrating violently, falling in a lifeless heap on the ground. Bill pointed his lighter at the guards. "Depart now or I will kill you too!" Bill was dying to say, "Go ahead. Make my day," but it just didn't sound the same in Hebrew.

They both turned running into the city as fast as they could. When they were out of sight, Bill looked down at his friend and smiled. "They're gone."

Opening his eyes, Kabe returned the smile. "How did I do?"

"You did great!" Bill joyfully replied. "I think you've watched some of the same T.V. shows I have."

"I do not understand this T.V. show," Kabe said. "You must live in a very strange time."

"It is a strange time, Kabe, but I still want to go back. We'd better hurry. It won't be long before those two guards discover they've been tricked, and the king is alive and well. Unfortunately, many others will be back when they hear the news. I can easily fly you to any part of the world to avoid these people. So where would you like to go?" Bill asked as he opened the hatch and began stowing his gear.

Kabe staggered back. "Me? Fly? I take my chances here on ground. I can outmaneuver temple guards. You better leave soon. When those two men discover I was on the sly, they be back ready to kill us on sight."

Bill wanted to explain to Kabe about the comet and what will happen, but Kabe's unwillingness to fly spelled no possible means of escaping the oncoming deluge for his friend. All efforts to change Kabe's mind failed as precious time slipped away.

"Take care of yourself," Bill reluctantly said. "You saved my life, and I am forever grateful to you." Bill stretched out his hand and so did Kabe. Tears welled up in Bill's eyes as he handed Kabe his lighter back and prepared to enter the Light Assimilator. He was certain what Kabe's fate would be in the next few days. If the king's men didn't get him, the oncoming catastrophe would.

Bill waved with a teary-eyed smile while closing the hatch. Activating the panels, he taxied down the path in an easterly direction. The newly risen sun emitted an ample amount of light to power the craft in the morning sky. Bill circled the area one last time with plans of going to the Middle East. He glanced down to see Kabe with his lighter in hand and the flame rising high. Bill quickly reached for one in the ship and returned the gesture tilting the wings back and forth as a wave goodbye. Soon Kabe was out of sight, but Bill could not get him out of his mind. If it had not been for this one brave soul, his life would have surely ended at the hands of King Pepi II.

CHAPTER FIFTEEN

Bill's new found freedom gave him a chance to begin deliberating his future. This marked day six of his confinement in this time. His earlier calculations indicated he had up to ten days from his arrival before the comet's tail changed the complexion of the earth forever. The "up to" part is what bothered him. The comet's blazing illumination could now be seen during the day. It enhanced the daytime leaving the entire population of the world questioning what would happen. Bill's intuition told him there may be only a day or two left before the Earth would be hit by a catastrophic deluge of ice.

According to the vibrations the ship encountered before it disengaged from light speed, the water belt's demise should take 30 to 60 days to rain down on the earth. On his trip back in time, the centrifugal force of being in light speed carried him through that rain-laden time span for two or three seconds. He doubted if his ship could remain airborne in conventional flight when the flood of water commenced falling. He calculated the rain should be heaviest at the start of this cataclysm and taper off as the days pass. In his judgment, the best option entailed locating the highest mountain in the world and waiting there until the water belt had dissipated allowing him to lift off and zip back to light speed. It sounded pretty good, assuming he could locate a suitable landing area at a high elevation where he wouldn't get washed down the mountainside during the torrential rains. To carry out this plan, copious amounts of rations would be needed for nourishment. He would also have to make sure his water supply was well stocked.

"I guess there will be an ample supply of fresh water falling right outside my window if I run short," Bill said with a smile as he flew over Palestine nearing the Dead Sea region.

Much to Bill's surprise, the Dead Sea wasn't dead at all! The lake now positioned itself above sea level. The Jordan River flowed in from the north and also flowed out the south streaming towards the east finger of what will shortly become the Red Sea. The mountains that earlier surrounded the Dead Sea hid themselves under the plush green rolling hills. Bill then recalled he had not seen any significant mountain ranges during this stop in time. "Surely I'll find something," he reassured himself adjusting his heading easterly in the direction of the fertile valley of the Tigris and Euphrates Rivers where ample food supplies undoubtedly abounded.

Recalling the scripture he'd been reading a few days earlier, he remembered that the alleged Garden of Eden was located in that area at the headwaters of four rivers. In modern days, only the Tigris and Euphrates flowed into the Persian Gulf, so his chances of finding anything were pretty slim. "If there is any semblance of truth to this legend, the region should at least provide a bountiful harvest of the provisions I am looking for."

Bill located a wide river resembling the Euphrates River on his maps and began following it upstream. Intermittent villages dotted the banks of the great river. Bill could not afford another human confrontation like he experienced in Egypt, so he continued his search for a suitable unpopulated place to land. Ahead, a major city spread out on the north bank of the river. "According to the map, that should be the ancient city of Babylon."

Time slipped away as Bill desperately needed to restock his food supply for the duration of the upcoming deluge. In the distance, Bill could see a major river flowing to the northwest.

"That must be the Tigris." He nodded in approval glancing at his charts. "Maybe I can find a deserted place around there to land." Bill raised his eyebrows as he saw a river flowing to the south and another one to the northeast. Neither of them showed up on any of his current maps. Fumbling through his papers, he located a remote map of the area. It indicated the northern stream to be called the Karun River. The southern river was not shown on the map, but it did indicate a valley or old river bed called the Wadi Rimah or the Wadi Batin. Bill decided to increase his altitude and get a better overview of the terrain. Once he gained altitude he viewed the area. Sure enough, the four rivers appeared to flow from one large river dividing into these four rivers!

Bill lowered his altitude resuming his search for a suitable place to land. Surprisingly, when he crossed over the last two rivers flowing from this great river, the signs of man astonishingly disappeared. An opening, relatively close to the river, materialized below him. He circled the area scanning the landscape for a trace of human life. The absence of human inhabitants in this location seemed odd but true, so he decided to attempt a landing. The craft wildly bounced over the rutty terrain coming to rest adjacent to this immense river.

His clock registered 4:00 PM. He knew by the time he foraged for sufficient amounts of food, it would be too late to travel anywhere else today. This locale, more than likely, would be his campsite for the night. Rigging up four containers out of materials in the ship, he proceeded downstream to gather foodstuffs. The river provided a focal point and directional means back to his vessel. It would be imperative to keep the river within his bearings at all times.

Immediately, all forms of fruits and berries unfolded. "Unfortunately these may not keep for a very long time since I won't have room to refrigerate much of it," Bill stated as he filled one of the containers. He discovered a patch of green vegetation resembling potatoes. Digging down he found the starchy carbohydrates needed to sustain his diet. They were a little green, but they'd do the trick. Filling his remaining make-shift buckets, he carried the cumbersome load back to the ship. This adventure reminded Bill of a scavenger hunt because he never knew what he'd find next.

The next trip down the river he discovered a thicket of ripe, juicy raspberries. While munching on the delectable fruit, he noticed a glowing light through the trees. The light resembled that of a fire, yet it didn't appear to be consuming anything. Bill cautiously moved closer to investigate. He didn't want to alert any of the local inhabitants of his presence and definitely didn't need any more delays like he'd encountered in Egypt.

Once at the edge of the forest, Bill's eyes widened in astonishment. Across a 30 meter clearing began an immaculately groomed orchard and garden. The river he'd been following ran through the middle of this groomed area. On the foremost edge of this area, an angelic creature was holding what appeared to be a large flaming sword guarding the path entering this paradise! Remembering his camera, Bill got it out to capture a few snapshots of the being. As Bill stood up to get a clear shot, the creature took note of his presence.

"Come forward!" demanded the being in a loud Hebrew voice. Bill's feet wanted to run the opposite direction, but the mystical reason for the creature being there drew him closer. Bill intently observed the non-consuming fire engulfing the being's sword as he stepped clear of the underbrush. Once in the open, the being demanded, "Why are you here? Do you not know this place is forbidden to all man?"

Bill, trying to be reverent, got down on one knee and replied, "I am from a land far away. I was not aware of the presence of this place. What can I tell my people is the name of this great haven?"

The creature replied very factually, "You know in your heart what this place is called. You have heard the story told by your ancestors many times, but your people do not listen, they do not believe."

Bill was not sure what he was talking about, but continued asking questions. "Why must you protect this area?"

"You still act as if you do not know." The creature rebuked him. "Your ancestors could have lived forever but gave in to the words of the tempter. For this reason, man does not have access to the Tree of Life or this beautiful garden. Now, you must go. It will not be long before man's woes begin and the time of this place will be no more."

With that, the being and the flaming sword faded into nothingness. Bill felt numb as he wandered back to camp. He surmised what the creature had referred to, but didn't want to believe it.

That night, around the fire, he retrieved Michelle's Bible from the ship and began reading in the second chapter of Genesis, "The Garden of Eden was located in the East. A river watering the garden flowed from Eden; it had four headstreams. The name of the first is the Pishon; it winds through the entire land of Havilah, where there is gold. The name of the second river is the Gihon; it winds through the entire land of Cush. The name of the third river is the Tigris; it runs along the east side of Asshur. And the fourth river is the Euphrates."

He went on to read how Adam and Eve fell to the temptation of Satan by eating of the Tree of the Knowledge of Good and Evil. For that sin, man was banned from the Garden and would be forced to work the soil for his survival. By the sweat of his brow shall he live. As for woman, she will always be dominated by man and will have great pain and troubles in child birth. For this great sin, man will be doomed to die and will not have the pleasure of immortality. For this reason a cherubim, the second highest ranking in the angels, will be placed in front of the Garden with a flaming sword to keep man from reentering the Garden and eating of the Tree of Life.

Bill sat in a state of shock. Everything matched exactly with the writings of the old book. He tried to sleep that night, but a restful slumber eluded him. The comet's luminosity lit up the night like another moon as it bore down on the earth and its inhabitants. Bill knew he needed to find a suitable mountain top very soon. The coasting factor had apparently been affected by the deteriorating water belt. Bill's best guess indicated he might have one more day before the comet delivered its crippling blow.

CHAPTER SIXTEEN

The morning came much too early for a man who had tossed and turned on the hard ground all night. Refreshed or not, Bill slowly picked himself up and started on the day's activities. After gathering four more loads of fruits and vegetables, Bill realized he would tire of this diet quickly. He intended to save the non-perishables for the end of the duration leaving him only the fresh fruits and vegetables for as long as they would keep. The tomatoes looked appealing when he picked them, but now he realized they'd only stink up the ship and rot in the next few days so he tossed them toward the edge of the forest.

Remembering his fishing adventure from his earlier stop, Bill decided to give it a try again. Things weren't quite as easy this time. After several misses and falling in the river, Bill returned to camp with a fine catch. Who knows what species of fish this one was? Its markings were different than Bill had ever seen.

The filet cooked slowly over the remaining coals of the night's fire while Bill changed his clothes and finished loading the Light Assimilator. The fish tasted good, but Bill found his appetite diminished. The events of the day before and the thought of the events to come left a knot in his churning stomach.

Just then, he heard the sound of someone or something coming up behind him! He turned quickly to see a small brachiosaurus munching on the tomatoes thrown by the edge of the forest. Bill's quick movement sent the little guy scurrying back into the woods. Bill quietly walked over to the ship grabbing the recorder. Sitting motionlessly next to the craft, he waited for the prehistoric creature to reemerge. Soon the small khaki colored dinosaur, about the size of a large cow, wandered out of the forest and continued feasting on the tomatoes.

Dinosaurs, being reptiles, did not depend on their parents to survive, according to Professor Berman. Once they hatched from their eggs, they were on their own. That thought eliminated the idea of mamma being close behind. He looked kind of cute and loveable.

"I think I'll call him Dino," Bill said with a smile thinking back to his childhood days of watching The Flintstones. Ever so slowly, Bill stood up and made his way toward the hungry little guy as the camera captured the event. "If they eat like this all the time, it's no wonder they grow to be so huge," Bill thought as he cautiously advanced.

Noting the approaching human, Dino lumbered back in the forest. Bill quickly picked up one of the tomatoes and followed Dino into the wooded area. Bill's new friend retreated into the dense trees following a path three meters wide. Dino's hurried waddle maintained a 20 meter lead ahead of Bill's persistent pursuit. Periodically Dino turned to view Bill's progress. Each time Bill held up the tomato calling the animal like a pet dog, "Here Dino, come here Dino. Look at this sweet juicy tomato I have just for you."

When the young dinosaur reached the next clearing, he stopped and turned around looking at this stranger bearing delectable food. Bill, still holding the tomato in one hand and his camera in the other, paused, and then slowly walked in the direction of the shy creature filming as he advanced. Surprisingly, Dino began walking back towards Bill. For some unknown reason, Dino gained courage when he entered the clearing. Bill stood perfectly still just on the edge of the trees allowing Dino to move in the last few steps and snatch the tomato right out of his hand. Having the whole escapade on tape Bill remarked, "This will make a great home video to show my children someday, if I ever get back to have any kids."

Bill lowered the camera from his eyes still pondering why his little friend decided to stop running and came back for the tomato. Suddenly, a gigantic brachiosaurus head dropped from the tops of the trees not more than ten meters away from Bill and let out a thunderous bellow!

Bill's terrified scream echoed for miles as his feet hurriedly carried him back through the forest.

"So that's what gave Dino the courage he needed. It may not have been mom or dad, but it was one of his own," Bill reasoned as he sped past the trees along the path. Unfortunately, this beast didn't like someone invading his territory. The five ton monster shook the ground with each step stomping his way through the forest in hot pursuit of this intruder. The welcomed sight of his glistening craft appeared through the trees nearing the edge of the forest. Luckily the hatch on the Light Assimilator remained open from being loaded earlier.

The vibrations escalated as the beast closed in on its enemy. Bill broke into a full sprint as he hit the clearing and turned for the ship. Halfway through the opening, he glanced back to access his adversary's progress. Inevitably, a piece of Bill's firewood seemingly jumped out in front of him, and Bill went sprawling face first on the ground next to the hot coals of his fire. He rolled over just in time to see a large flat foot preparing to descend upon his frail body. With a crushing blow, the 10,000 pound reptile hurtled its foot in Bill's direction only to find the remainder of his fire grinding hot coals in the bottom of his foot. The deafening sound emitted by the enraged monster could be heard throughout the forest as Bill scrambled to his feet. Rushing to his ship, he frantically dove inside. The furious brachiosaurus boiled with anger as he eyed the small ship and prepared to attack. Hurriedly fumbling with the controls, Bill tried to adjust the correct switches as this killer approached. The mad dinosaur spun around to swat the little ship with his huge tail just as Bill activated the panels on the Light Assimilator.

A mighty swinging blow of the reptile's tail barely caught the rear rudder of the ship spinning Bill around like a top. He came to rest aimed directly at the creature. There was no possible way to take off pointing this direction, so Bill attempted to steer clear of the monster and by all means avoid the reach of that powerful tail. The brachiosaurus stood directly in the middle of the takeoff area forcing Bill to circle the creature, making certain he maintained a safe distance. At the far end of the clearing Bill stopped the ship pointing toward the monster.

Opening the hatch and sticking his head out he yelled, "Hey dragon breath, your mamma was a salamander!"

Clearly seeing the human again brought the creature on with a charge and away from the middle of the takeoff strip. The ship swerved around the oncoming reptile as Bill taxied down the clearing and took off into the morning sky. Circling the furious beast, he took a couple more pictures as evidence of this memorable adventure.

Bill's heart pounded from his morning workout. He hoped he hadn't left anything important at the campsite. If he had, he certainly wasn't going back after it! Unfortunately, the coals of the fire remained red hot and scattered from the dinosaur's activities. "If a forest fire starts due to my inability to douse the coals, it won't be long before it will get washed out," Bill reasoned.

The next order of business involved locating a high mountain suitable for landing. After studying his maps, Bill decided to head north toward the Caucasus Mountain Range. He followed the Tigris River north and west to help lead him to the range. This marked day number seven of his stay in 2351 B.C. while the comet closed in by the minute.

About 100 miles upstream Bill glanced down catching sight of something shocking his senses. From the air, it looked like a long barracks house with wood siding. In the last 3000 years, he had not encountered any buildings with split wood siding. He circled the structure descending to get a closer look. The enormous structure stretched longer than a football field. Then came the biggest surprise of all, it wasn't a building!

"It can't be!" Bill exclaimed exuberantly. At that moment, he didn't care what risks were involved. He was going to land the ship and investigate this wonder.

CHAPTER SEVENTEEN

Acres of harvested forest land left abundant choices for a landing strip. In an attempt to avoid any more human confrontations, Bill parked his ship a mile from the destination. After camouflaging the craft and stuffing his 35mm camera under his robe, he began walking. If this structure is what he thought it was, he didn't care when the comet struck as long as he had the opportunity to view this piece of history.

A quarter of a mile from the location his doubts vanished concerning what he had discovered. Before him rested the mystically renowned Ark sitting on dry land next to the Tigris River! Bill had to take a picture from this location to encompass the entire structure's width. There didn't seem to be any people in the vicinity, so Bill concealed his camera back under his robe moving in for a closer inspection. The mammoth size of this vessel amazed Bill. He could not believe that a man without modern tools could possibly construct anything this enormous. The rectangular wooden housing rested atop a boat-like floating device curved up at each end. The flattened curved ends would work like a weather vane in the wind helping the ship to turn into the waves. The lower section was partially below the plateau of the surface. A huge trench surrounding the structure revealed the remainder of the ship awaiting the oncoming flood of water. The floating device was covered with a gray matter similar to stucco or cement. It did not appear to be covering a smooth wood surface. The wavy lines that stretched up the side walls and ran the length of the ship created more questions concerning the vessels construction.

arches of the sun from sun up to sun down, we will provide him with enough food to feed him and his family for four seasons."

"You mean the pyramids weren't built by slaves?" Bill interrupted.

"Absolutely not!" exclaimed the king. "Slaves are not dependable. They do not do acceptable work. Slaves may be able to do the menial jobs, but they could never be trusted to do the actual construction of such a masterpiece as a great pyramid! On a project of the magnitude of the great pyramids, you need men who take pride in their work. The men also knew if they did not do a good job, they would not be rehired anytime in the future."

"How many men did you use at a time?" Bill asked.

"On the large pyramids we used approximately 25,000 men at a time. On a project like the Sphinx, we only used 5,000 men. And I already know your next question, how long did it take to build. The largest pyramid took 120 seasons to build," he stated factually.

Bill quickly divided by four indicating 30 years of construction. Bill's hunger for knowledge kept the questions flowing. "How were you able to build these massive structures with only hand tools? Also, how were you able to be so precise in calculating your measurements for the great pyramids?"

"We learned perfection from our mistakes. If you look around the countryside, you will see our early failures by Pharaoh Zoser. King Seneferu, Chephren, and Khufu (otherwise known as Cheops) learned how to build these structures and at what angles we could construct them. We quickly realized the structures must be perfectly square. To accomplish this, we fabricated four long strands of rope out of reeds exactly the same length. Then we calculated what the diagonal length should be and made two more strands that length. From those ropes, we formulated a perfectly square base for the pyramid. We wanted to point the Sphinx directly toward the rising sun in mid-season and wanted the pyramids to face the same direction."

"We also found it is imperative we have a level rock base to commence building the pyramid on. The laborers chisel trenches in the rock at the parameter of the structure. We then pour water in the channels measuring the depths of the water. This process enables

Massive anchor stones strategically sat around the perimeter of the Ark. There were cabled to the deck above with heavy twisted reeds coated with a waterproofing substance. Nearing one of the stones, he could see it stood over seven feet tall.

"This stone must weigh a ton!"

Faint noises caught Bill's attention. He wheeled around to find no one there. Listening closer revealed the sounds came from within the Ark! A closer examination revealed the rumblings of animals. Slowly walking to the end of the Ark, he heard everything from cows to elephants to who-knows-what.

From the end, the structure appeared to be over a city block long. Bill thought stepping it off would give him a better idea of its dimensions. Counting his paces he walked the entire length of the Ark. "One hundred seventy-two paces translates into approximately 516 feet," Bill said writing down the figure on a notebook pad hidden in his robe pocket. Looking up, he judged the height to be 50 feet with a small opening at the top of the Ark. The opening descended a couple feet from the top of the wooden structure and ran the entire length of the Ark on both sides.

On the other side of the vessel, Bill discovered what looked to be an enormous door in the middle of the Ark. The door had no outside handles or hinges, but it had to be the door since no other openings could be found.

Bill was admiring the construction of the vessel when a Hebrew voice from behind remarked, "Crazy people. Can't understand what they're doing in there."

Bill whirled around to find a local inhabitant coming right at him. He was a bearded man with fair complexion about 6' 4" tall wearing a cloth-like robe similar to Bill's. He didn't seem wary of Bill's presence or notice anything different about Bill's appearance and just kept rattling on about this big boat.

"This man spent half his life building this boat," the local continued, "then locks himself and his family inside with a bunch of animals."

"Who is this man?" Bill asked already knowing the answer, but wanting confirmation.

The man looked at Bill for a second and replied, "You must be new to this area. This Noah guy got the idea a long time ago that his God planned on sending water over all the land. His God told him to build this boat. He went to many different peoples trying to convince them to believe him, but everyone knew he was insane. Noah and his three sons, Ham, Shem, and Japheth have been working on this thing forever. From the time they started, I have fathered 27 sons and acquired vast herds and riches, while he has nothing."

"What about the animals?" Bill questioned. "How many did he take and how did he get them in there?"

"You should have been here. People came from all around these parts to witness this spectacle. Using the big door as a ramp, they loaded up enough food and supplies to last seasons. They must have used up half of one of the three floors just for foodstuffs. Then the animals began coming. Groups of seven clean animals and pairs of unclean animals all came and loaded themselves on the Ark. He even took behemoth with him!"

Behemoth couldn't fit through the door, could he?" Bill exclaimed.

"He took baby ones," the local explained. "I guess he wanted to be fair and get some of everything. I can't think of any animals he didn't get. Then after all the animals were on board and in their pens, Noah and his wife, his three sons and their wives, went inside. Somehow, after that, the door closed itself!"

"How long ago did all this occur?" If Bill remembered correctly the scripture stated how many days Noah remained locked in the Ark before the rains came.

The local stopped to think for a minute. "It has been five or six arches of the great light since they went inside and the door was closed," he replied confidently. He began questioning how Bill could not know anything about the plight of Noah and his great farce. "Where do you hail from and what tribe do you belong to?" demanded the local.

Bill thought fast and responded, "I come from the land south of the Great Sea. I belong to the Tribe of Kabe under the rule of the King Pepi II. We had heard this great vessel was under construction and I have been sent to investigate."

The answer satisfied the local causing Bill to heave a silent sigh of relief. The last thing he needed now was another confrontation. "This would be a good time to make my exit," Bill muttered under his breath as he began moving away from the local. "I must leave now and report back to my people," Bill said as he vanished around the corner of the Ark. He quickly rounded the bow of the ship, or was it the stern? He couldn't tell the front from the back, but it didn't matter. Out of the local's sight, he jogged the remainder of the way back to his craft. He was relieved to find his ship had sat undetected during his adventurous encounter. For once, his stop went off without a hitch.

Back in the air, he picked up Michelle's Bible to confirm everything he had witnessed and learned. The dimensions of the Ark listed in the sixth chapter of Genesis were 300 cubits long, 50 cubits wide and 30 cubits high.

"What is a cubit?" Bill asked as he fired up his international dictionary on the computer. Cubits were not of a universal length. They differentiated from country to country. A Hebrew cubit measured 18 inches. "That would have made the Ark 450 feet long. Why the difference?" He recalled his father's teachings how Moses wrote the first five books of the Bible. Moses learned all his construction techniques in Egypt. Bill glanced back in his dictionary to find an Egyptian cubit measuring 20.6 inches. A quick calculation determined a distance of 515 feet.

The scripture went on to state that the Ark had three floors, a door on one side, and a one cubit wide window running the length of the Ark. It took Noah and his three sons 120 years to build it. Noah constructed the vessel out of gopher wood and covered it with pitch to make it waterproof. Bill looked up gopher wood on his computer. The original word from the Hebrew text was not translatable. They were not even sure if it was a tree but some form of a growing plant.

Noah took seven of all clean animals and two of all other animals. Noah, his wife, Ham, Shem, Japheth, and their wives entered the Ark and the Lord shut the door. And the Lord said, "Seven days from now I will release the waters from under the earth and the waters from the heavens for 40 days and 40 nights upon the earth, and I will wipe from the face of the earth every living creature that I have made." Bill went on to read, "The waters rose greatly on the earth and all the high mountains under the entire heavens were covered. The waters rose and covered the highest mountains to a depth of more than 20 feet."

At this point, Bill slowly closed the Bible gently placing it behind him while staring into space. His ultimate plan had been to locate the highest mountain and ride out the storm. Up until now, every fact the Bible stated turned out to be true. Now it indicated the highest mountain would be covered with at least 20 feet of water. If Genesis proved to be true, his plan was destined to fail, and he was sentenced to die along with every other living creature on the earth. "But there is no way the water could cover 29,000 foot mountains," Bill reasoned.

His maps indicated the Ararat Mountain Range should be ahead. All Bill could see were rolling hills and a few plateaus. Bill flew lower with the elevation reading in his craft under 5,000 feet. Bill now recalled he had not seen any high mountains in the Middle East since the water belt was in place.

"The high mountain ranges must emerge after the ice clamps down on the earth," Bill deduced from his findings. That is why the water coming on the earth will be able to cover all the current mountains to a depth of 20 feet! My only hope may depend on the thickness of the water belt. Before the flood reaches my location, I can attempt to get airborne and remain in flight until the water belt vanishes, if there is enough light."

This theory appeared to be the only option Bill had. He chuckled when he thought of trying to land his craft on top of the Ark to ride out the storm, but the pitch roof on the Ark made that impossible. "It's too bad I hadn't listened to Michael's suggestion of having some alternate form of power to fly the ship. Then I may have had a remote chance of remaining in the air, allowing the water belt to dissipate and permitting ample amounts of ultraviolet rays to power his craft once again." Bill knew the initial raging downpour would be much too torrent for the ship to withstand in the air.

Totally frustrated Bill remarked, "It's too bad I can't call on my cell phone or send Michael a letter telling him to come back and get me." At that moment, a small glimmer of hope entered Bill's mind as his eyes lit up. "Why didn't I think of that earlier!" he exuberantly exclaimed turning the ship around and heading South.

CHAPTER EIGHTEEN

The last five weeks since Bill's departure crept by like the hour hand on the grandfather clock for Michael and Becky in Riverside. Each day they kept thinking, this would be the day Bill returned home. Nerves and optimism wore thin as the strain of the situation took its toll.

"Michael, it's been over a month since Bill left," Becky said factually as they prepared for bed. "We must face the fact that he isn't coming back. The kids are scheduled to begin school next week in Kansas City. We can't force them to change schools and friends just because you want to wait around for someone who may never return."

Michael knew Becky's assumption was probably correct. Bill surely would have returned by now if indeed he was coming back. Reluctantly he agreed to lock up the house and return to their rented home in Kansas City. "First thing in the morning we will inform the kids and start packing," Michael agonizingly conceded as they crawled in bed.

The idea of leaving Bill lost in time greatly disturbed Michael. Lying in bed, he stared at the ceiling wondering what could have conceivably gone awry. Then came the realization that someone should explain Bill's disappearance to the authorities. Certainly they would lock Michael up and throw away the key if he attempted to convince them Bill traveled back in time.

"Why didn't he leave me the plans to build one of those things? Maybe I could have at least proven to the authorities how he left this world," Michael thought. He had searched the files of Bill's computer to no avail. All Michael had seen Bill with was notebooks and architectural papers. Disheartened and discouraged, he drifted off to sleep.

A startling shrill ring of the telephone jolted Michael and Becky out of bed at 3:00 A.M. "Who could that possibly be?" questioned Michael groggily as they stumbled into the kitchen.

Becky got there first sleepily answering the phone. Holding her hand over the other ear she replied, "Yes he is. Who is this?" An eerie silence filled the kitchen as Becky strained to listen to the response. With a confused look on her face, she covered the receiver on the phone and asked Michael, "Do you know a Pierre Neesto from Iraq?"

Surprisingly, Michael remembered he had heard that French name. He and Bill had discussed a dig Pierre was beginning near Babylon. He grabbed the phone from Becky. "This is Michael Hansen." The next few minutes were filled with an agonizing silence for Becky as Michael intently listened to the Frenchman. Finally, Michael spoke, "Yes I will. Thank you for calling." With a bewildered look on his face, he handed the phone back to Becky to be hung up. Slowly he sat down in the kitchen chair staring at the floor.

"Well, what's this all about?" She asked.

"They want me to come to Baghdad," Michael replied quietly continuing his steady gaze at the floor.

Becky powerfully grabbed him by the shoulders forcing him to look at her. "What's going on Michael?"

Looking into her eyes, Michael meekly replied, "You'd better sit down for this one, honey. This Frenchman, Pierre Neesto, is a well-known archeologist. He is currently in charge of a dig near the site of the ancient city of Babylon. He said he found my experiment and is willing to fly me over there if I explain to him the purpose of it and how I duped his dating equipment!"

"What experiment?" Becky butted in. "They must have the wrong Michael Hansen."

"While excavating the base of the outer wall of the old city, their metal detectors located a large metal object. Supposedly, during this age, most metals were not known. Gradually sifting through the ancient soil, they found a long metal box 24 inches long and 10 inches wide. It looks very similar to a modern day tool box and is completely covered with a sticky matter they believe started out to be a tape-like substance able to keep moisture out of the box. Before opening the container, they time dated the soil discovering it to be 7,000 years old. Cautiously, Pierre opened the box to find a notebook taped shut along the edges with modern day duct tape. Indentations on the cardboard notebook cover read,

> "DO NOT OPEN. THIS IS AN EXPERIMENT. RETURN TO MICHAEL HANSEN, 6511 Magnolia Avenue, Riverside, California, U.S.A. 92501 Phone: 714-555-3208 AT ANY COST PLEASE RETURN THIS MATERIAL. YOU WILL BE COMPENSATED GREATLY."

Stillness enveloped the kitchen as they stared at each other with questioning eyes. "I've got to go, Becky, and find out what is in that notebook. You know as well as I do who that came from. If nothing else, this may explain to us what went wrong. Pierre has a plane ticket waiting for me at the airport. If you agree, I'll be leaving in the morning."

Becky reluctantly nodded her head yes. "What will you tell Pierre?"

"I don't know," Michael replied softly. "Hopefully I'll think of something. I can understand his confusion finding something made in the last ten years and date testing 7,000 years old."

The long flight wore on Michael's stressed mind and body. Michael thought he'd have plenty of time to formulate an explanation for Pierre, but his concentration focused on what message would be contained in the notebook. Twenty hours later and a couple plane changes, Michael landed in Baghdad. The Iraqi August sun beat down on Michael as he departed his flight and walked to the terminal. Inside the airport stood a small-framed man with dry, weathered skin holding a sign, "MICHAEL HANSEN".

Extending his hand to the gentleman Michael stated, "I am Michael Hansen."

"I am Pierre Neesto," came the accented response from the Frenchman. "I am very happy you were able to come on such short notice. I am extremely interested in your experiment and how you apparently fooled my devices."

"I hope we did not cause any delays or problems for you or your men," Michael said. "My partner, Bill Abrams, and I are very interested in the results of your tests."

"You must explain your methods and reasons for the experiment. I ran every test imaginable on this container and kept deducting the same results. If this metal box is not 7,000 years old, then how did you cause it to register as such?" Pierre asked.

"Let me examine the contents of the container. Then I will explain everything," promised Michael. Under his breath he added, "I hope."

Pierre's jeep waited to transport them to the dig site located 100 miles south and east of Baghdad. During the journey, the two men traded stories on archeological finds and studies. As Pierre spoke, Michael recalled numerous articles written about Mr. Neesto and his discoveries. His expertise in this field would hamper Michael's chances of convincing Pierre this so-called experiment was real.

Pierre seemed impressed by the work Michael had been associated with the past few years indicating he would be starting a dig back in the States the next year. Pierre asked, "If you were interested in working with us, I'd be more than happy to commission you and your partner for my venture."

"Thank you," Michael graciously acknowledged. "I will have to discuss that with my associate and get back to you." All Michael really hoped for was a chance to discuss anything with his associate and friend.

The journey over the primitive roads took much longer than Michael had anticipated. The lack of air conditioning in these hot and arid conditions took its toll. The anxiety of what awaited him made the tedious voyage that much longer. At long last, the excavation site located on the north banks of the Euphrates River appeared over the ridge. Pierre's workforce included two dozen men meticulously taking up the soil and sifting it to extract any artifacts. Michael observed the outer wall of the ancient city uncovered beneath ground level.

"Exactly where did you find the container?" Michael inquired.

A look of confusion spread across Pierre's face. "You should know. You put it there."

Michael thought fast and responded somewhat tongue-tied, "Oh, well, see, my partner Bill was the one who buried the container. I was on assignment at the time. He never did tell me precisely where it was located." Michael rolled his eyes in relief as Pierre nodded his-head in agreement and led him toward the site where the container was found. Ahead, Michael could see a two meter square area roped off.

"This is the place," Pierre announced. "With our detectors we discovered the presence of a large metal object beneath the surface. Before digging, we did a compaction study on the soil in this area. The test indicated the ground had not been disturbed in centuries. Excitement grew as the men painstakingly sifted their way to the large metal object. We were certain we had discovered a metallic substance in an area and an era where metal was not known. The men anticipated possible treasures of gold and silver. They were disappointed when we discovered a box with only a notebook in it, but I am all the more perplexed by this experiment. Please share with me your secrets."

Michael knew he had to begin satisfying Pierre's questions or he may not be able to obtain what he came for. "Thirteen months ago my partner discovered the possibility of this site existing. After our surface ultrasound testing had been completed, we agreed we had located the outer wall of the old city. My partner developed a compound that ages material quickly and needed to test it. The compound reacts with the elements in the ground after it has been exposed to the soil for approximately one year. We were confident an expert like yourself would be assigned to a project of this magnitude. We were assured a professional archeologist discovering an artifact under these circumstances would test it in every way imaginable to determine its age. By doing this, we have obtained a third party verification of the results of our test. You stated your tests concluded the container to be approximately 7,000 years old when it is actually less than ten. Speaking for my partner and myself, I would conclude this process to be a success!"

"What is this substance?" Pierre asked. "And what about the soil not having previously being disturbed?"

"It is an acid-like compound that reacts with the nitrogen in the soil. That is the reason the compound must be exposed to the dirt for a period of time. As he replaced the soil around the container, small amounts of the compound were applied to each layer and then compacted. A generous dose covered the top. In a matter of months, the area appeared relatively undisturbed except for the lack of long term growing plants," Michael explained. "I hope you can understand if I do not reveal the ingredients of the substance at this time."

Michael paused for a moment awaiting a reaction from Pierre. His delayed nod of approval prompted Michael to add, "And as the notebook indicates, we will gladly compensate you and your men for the hours and expenses incurred from locating this object."

Pierre responded amiably, "In the past I have given many items people told me were very old, and I was able to prove them wrong. Here I find an item that is modern, yet my instruments lie to me. You have fooled the old expert. You do not owe me anything because you have taught me that I am not perfect. Now, I will take you to your items, but first answer me one more question.

Michael held his breath while nodding his head.

"If you and your partner discovered the outer walls of this ancient city, why didn't you claim the find and begin the excavation here?" Pierre awaited his response.

He had a good question. Michael paused momentarily gathering his thoughts. "At the time we discovered this site, we had already been commissioned by the U.S. government to do the ice cap study in Barrow, Alaska. We knew if we backed out on the contract, we would never receive a U.S. appointment again and it would tarnish our work credit rating. We would have loved to be the archeologists who gained the credit for this discovery, but our business sense told us it would be better in the long run to work the Alaska job first. Besides, there existed the slim chance no one would locate this site by the time we finished there. That scenario proved to be our ultimate dream, but it did not materialize."

Pierre considered that to be a pretty good answer. Michael thought it was a pretty good answer too, smiling as he followed Pierre across the compound! Entering one of the huge tents, Pierre directed Michael to a clear rectangle showcase. Inside rested what looked like Bill's toolbox coated with dried on duct tape.

"We left the notebook inside the container just as we found it," Pierre stated. "We did not open the notebook in accordance with the instructions on the cover. The vacuum sealed case helps preserve the contents. But I guess that isn't necessary now since you have confirmed this item is not a Babylonian artifact." Releasing the vacuum and unlocking the case, Pierre left the tent to return to his excavating.

Michael's hands trembled as he reached in the case and opened the lid on the toolbox. Inside, the corroded notebook lay still duct taped shut along the edges. The words and numbers on the cover had faded away with time. Luckily, the pen's deep impressions in the cardboard cover had enabled Pierre to decipher the message. But now came the possibility the words inside had faded also making it impossible to read. Michael's whole body quivered in anticipation as his knife slit the sticky edges of the tape opening the dry and aged notebook divulging its hidden contents. Michael's greatest fear became a reality as he opened to a blank page.

CHAPTER NINETEEN

Intermittent pen strokes dotted the page as Michael ran his shaking fingers over the rough page trying to discern what Bill's message revealed.

"If only my fingers could feel the letters." Michael's head raised as a determined stare scanned the room. Upon spotting his prey, he bounced from the chair retrieving a canister of pencils. Holding a pencil on its side, he lightly skimmed over the surface of the paper. Clear etchings where the graphite did not touch appeared on the page as words materialized. With the pulse rate of a sprinter, Michael finished tinting the page and prepared to read the manuscript.

> The date is August 16th in the year 2351 B.C. I am on top of one of the highest mountains in the Mt. Ararat region in Turkey trapped in time. I need your help. Your theory of the comet creating the Ice Age is correct. It will strike tomorrow. Before the Ice Age, the entire earth lived in a tropical paradise due to a water belt surrounding the earth above the sky as written in the first chapter of Genesis. Your last minute discovery concerning Methuselah was also correct. Due to the lack of radiation penetrating the water belt, man and animals live for hundreds of years. Everything you read in the Bible concerning early history I have found to be correct right down to Noah and the Ark! Because of the water belt, I am no longer able to time travel since the

water blocks the majority of the ultraviolet rays. When I encountered the existence of the belt, my ship coasted out of light speed eight days. Tomorrow, after the ice particles break through the northern and southern sections of the water belt, the remainder of the belt will be left to rain torrents on the earth for 40 days and 40 nights. My original plan consisted of holding out on the highest mountain until the belt is depleted, but the scripture states the flood waters will cover the highest mountain peak by 20 feet! Please believe me. The Bible is 100% correct from the Garden of Eden on down. I would tend to believe if its rendition of creation is correct, the rest of the scripture is probably also correct.

I need your help or I am doomed to die. In my basement safe are the plans for building the Light Assimilator. The combination is 30-15-42-15. I need you to construct a new ship and rescue me. I realize Becky may not want you to risk your life since I ran into such difficulty. If you can't, please try to find some young adventurer willing to take the risk. But you are the only one that knows the complexities and capabilities of this device. Besides, you are the only person that I can really trust.

There is one major alteration you will need to make in the design. It will require some form of a propelling device to keep us aloft through the torrential rains for 40 days. It may take a small nuclear motor to sustain that kind of power for that length of time. With the ship's present design, you can add up to 1000 pounds. Any weight above that will require extra length and wing span. Your physics should enable you to calculate the proportions. The money we acquired from Vegas should cover the construction costs, if you haven't spent it already.

I have so much to tell you and show you about the past. My questions have now all been answered. By the way, your theory on the land masses was also correct. They are currently bunched together waiting to move apart as written in the 10th chapter of Genesis during the time of Peleg.

Don't rush your end of the project. A year from the time you receive this would still enable you to return to rescue me. I'm the one who has to sweat out the next few days to see if you're coming or not. Remember the coasting factor. When you start vibrating violently in 2351 B.C. means you're in the torrential rains. Shut down then so you won't get back during the time of the water belt's dominance. I can survive the flood until it reaches the mountain tops.

May God's speed and blessing be with you.

P.S. Tell Michelle thanks for leaving her Bible with me. I would have never survived without it.

Tears of joy filled Michael's eyes as he reached the end of the letter. The one in a million chance of Bill's message reaching him had been successful. Now all Michael had to do was build a new and improved Light Assimilator, go back in time, and pick up his friend. The thought of his mechanical capabilities quickly sobered Michael's thoughts of rescue. "I'm no mechanic," reasoned Michael sliding down in the chair. "How can he expect me to construct this complicated device? I don't even change the oil in my own car! How could I possibly assemble a time machine?"

The long trip home gave Michael plenty of time to review his options. Michael knew Becky would not be in favor of him traveling back in time even if he could construct the thing. But, on the other hand, she wouldn't want him to leave Bill stranded in time. Her idea would probably be to send someone else to do it. So, how do you go about hiring someone to help build a time machine to travel 5000 years into the past and rescue someone from the Great Flood? Michael reasoned the only way he could convince anyone he had the capabilities of time travel was the same way Bill proved it to him. In his mind that left him no other choice than to construct the craft himself. Once assembled, he'd cross the bridge of who's going to get Bill. By this time, Los Angeles appeared on the horizon as the 747 began its descent.

The airport clock read 1:00 P.M. when Michael exited the building and hopped in a cab heading for home. Becky was the only one at the house when he arrived. The kids had gone to the pool for the afternoon. Instead of trying to explain the situation, he handed her the notebook.

When she had finished reading, she asked suspiciously, "What are you going to do?"

Michael realized the best chance of having his wife's blessing on the project would be if she made the final decision for him to proceed with Bill's request. "Well, what do you think I should do?"

A deafening silence filled the room as they stared at each other with questioning eyes. Becky finally broke the stillness. "If there is any chance of retrieving Bill safely, we have to try. He may be a crazy guy that leads you astray occasionally, but deep down he's an okay soul. We can't desert him now if we're his only hope."

These were the words Michael wanted to hear. Walking over to his wife, he embraced her kissing her on the cheek and whispering in her ear, "Thank you, I love you." Backing away he added, "And Bill loves you too!"

"Now just because I said you could pursue the project doesn't mean you can go!" Becky reasoned. "It means you can start building the craft. I would prefer someone else going on this daredevil mission."

"Yes mother," Michael replied heading towards the basement.

The next order of business involved locating the plans Bill alluded to. After five minutes of searching, a small gray safe materialized in the back of a basement closet. Giving the dial a few spins, Michael twirled the combination 30-15-42-15, and nothing happened. He tried it again with the same results. "Is it possible there's another safe in the house?" Michael frustratingly asked giving the handle a forceful jerk.

"Here, let me try a woman's touch," Becky calmly said kneeling down in front of the safe. "You southpaws are always backward. Did you try starting the dial in the opposite direction?"

Michael shrugged his shoulders not wanting to admit he hadn't thought of that. She wheeled the dial around, turned the handle, and "Bingo!" she proudly announced turning around sticking her tongue out at her husband.

All sorts of papers emerged from the safe ranging from a high school diploma to life insurance policies. "How would you like to file for Bill's life insurance and record his death on August 16, 2351 B.C.?" Michael said with a smile.

Becky didn't think that was very amusing. She kept her head in the safe pulling out more and more papers. Michael tried to examine everything she tossed on the floor. "That's all," she said turning around looking at the mixed up pile of papers on the floor. "Is it in there somewhere?"

"I don't see anything in here that resembles plans for anything!" Michael exclaimed. "Are you sure that's all there is inside the safe?"

"Look for yourself," Becky disgustingly replied moving out of the way so he could. take a look. Examining the safe, Michael found there wasn't as much as a paper clip remaining inside. "Where can it possibly be?" Michael asked with an anguished tone in his voice. "How can anyone lose something in a safe?"

Becky raised her eyebrows and commented, "What if he only thought he put it in the safe? Sometimes you've thrown your papers on the desk, later assuming you put them away in the desk."

Michael looked at her and thought this was no time to be discussing his neatness habits. Instead of saying anything, he began searching around the base of the safe. With a couple mighty tugs, he slid the safe a few inches from the wall wedging his hand back behind. The slight chance always existed Bill had thrown the papers on top and they slipped behind the safe. Michael's heart raced as he felt something like the edge of a notebook. "I think I've got something!" Michael excitedly hollered to Becky. A spiral notebook emerged in Michael's hand, just a plain student notebook with no markings what-so-ever on the outside.

Michael hesitated in fear anticipating another disappointment. He opened the red cover discovering a page full of mathematical calculations hodgepodge all over the page. It looked like Bill had problems balancing his checkbook. Michael flipped the page to reveal they had found what they were looking for. The heading read, "The Light Assimilator by William B. Abrams". Both Michael and Becky exhaled a sigh of relief. They had crossed the first hurdle in finding their friend. Unfortunately, this would be the easiest of the hurdles to clear.

CHAPTER TWENTY

Surprisingly, Bill's blueprints meticulously listed all the materials used in the construction of the craft. The step by step procedures seemed to make sense as Michael glanced over the pages. "This looks about as easy as that bicycle I put together for Michelle last Christmas!" Michael declared with a chuckle. Getting one of those looks from Becky he added, "I didn't have too many pieces left over when I got finished!"

"What about the parts? Do you have any idea where you can get everything you need?" Becky asked trying to get the discussion back on track.

Michael thought for a second. "If I correctly remember, there are a lot of spare parts left over in the garage. Let's go take a look."

The two of them bounced off the floor running up the stairs in anticipation of what they might find in the garage. Amidst the clutter and maze of tools, they discovered two huge wooden boxes filled with light panels and miscellaneous plane parts.

"Looks like we're in luck. Maybe all we'll need is a small plane body and one other item," Michael resounded.

"What other item?" Becky asked.

"Remember in Bill's letter he indicated I would need some form of long-term propelling device. He suggested a small nuclear motor, but there's no way I could get a hold of anything like that. I guess I'll have plenty of time to think about it while I finish the rest of the craft," Michael stated as he continued sorting through the available parts.

A rumbling sound in the house and the familiar sound of, "Mom, where are you?" told Michael and Becky the kids were home. Upon seeing their daddy, Michelle and Marty swarmed around him. Michael knelt down to a ton of hugs and kisses. He also received a bath from the wet swimsuits, but he didn't mind.

"What did you find out on your long trip daddy?" Michelle asked anxiously. "Is Bill coming home soon?"

"Bill isn't coming home just yet, honey," Michael responded as he looked at his concerned daughter. "He had a problem with his ship, so he wants daddy to build a new one to go and get him."

"Oh boy!" exclaimed Marty. "Can I go too? Please?"

"We don't even know if daddy will be the one to go," explained Michael. "We have to get it built first. Unfortunately, that will take quite a while and school starts back in Kansas City in a few days. You and your mother will need to return home while I stay here and finish."

"How come?" whined Michelle.

"All your friends are back there," reasoned Becky. "Besides, I'd have a good chance of going back to work at Park Valley."

"Oh Mom," complained Michelle. "You're a nurse. You can get a job anywhere. Besides, we've got the money Bill left us. We'd rather stay here with Daddy than go back to our friends right now, wouldn't we Marty."

Marty nodded his head up and down and up and down.

"So it's okay?" Michelle pleaded. "We can stay here until Daddy gets finished and Bill comes home?"

Becky and Michael looked at each other wondering what the other was thinking. "That sounds fine to me if it's okay with your mother," Michael said receiving a nod of approval from Becky. "But first we'll have to see if we can get you registered for school here. Then we'll know for sure."

The kids responded joyously bouncing around their folks. Cutting into their celebration, Michael asked, "By the way Michelle, did you know you left your Bible in Bill's ship?"

Apprehensive of her dad's intentions, Michelle cautiously looked up at her father nodding her head yes. "I thought Bill might have a lot of time to read on his trip. And since he didn't go to church, I believed it would be good for him."

"Well, Bill told me to tell you thank you," Michael replied proudly. "He's read part of it and said he thoroughly enjoyed it. That was very thoughtful of you." That statement brought on a big smile from Michelle as she scurried off to change her wet clothes.

The next few weeks involved locating a suitable plane body, sorting out parts, and most of all, trying to decipher Bill's notes. As the work continued, the problem of the long range motor weighed heavily on Michael's mind. A small nuclear motor similar to what the government had introduced last year seemed to be the only answer. This dilemma haunted Michael day and night as he labored to finish the Light Assimilator II. Unfortunately, he had to complete the craft before he added the motor. Michael realized he needed the finished product to prove to someone what he had.

After eight stressful weeks of 12-hour days, Michael produced an exact duplicate of the craft Bill departed in three months earlier. Now the big question remained whether it would work or not. Michael's uncertainty about his ability to construct such a machine left him hesitant to test it. His father owned a small plane when Michael was a teen allowing him to fly the craft on many occasions while transporting supplies. Michael was confident of his piloting ability, but his primary concern though, was whether he had constructed the craft correctly.

That evening, just after sunset, with the plane sitting in Bill's driveway, Michael climbed into the cockpit of the Light Assimilator II. He prepared to activate one of the light panels to see if the ship responded. The sun's disappearance over the horizon left a much lower concentration of ultraviolet rays for the panel to be attracted to. Any movement what-so-ever would constitute success in Michael's mind for this test. With a flip of the switch, the craft coasted down the driveway. Responding quickly, Michael shut down the panel, but the ship glided into the street! As luck would have it, a late model mid-size car sped in his direction. Cramping the front wheels of the craft Michael reactivated the light panel. The ship turned on a dime rolling back into the driveway avoiding the oncoming auto. The car swerved dangerously between the curbs as the driver stared at this strange contraption rolling in and out of the street. Michael quickly decided it would be best to keep this baby locked up in the garage until the time arrived to take it out in the desert for the final testing.

In the back of the design notebook, Bill had composed a complete novel on his theory how the craft should perform in time travel, indicating speeds and durations for different lengths of journeys. Short trips under 30 days could be programmed into the onboard computer system controlling time and place of reentry. These trips could be taken anywhere between the 45th Latitudes. Longer journeys had to be controlled manually giving the operator no control of the location of reentry. The theory concerning the coasting factor was also mentioned, which Bill had referenced in his letter. Michael took an additional three days to study these figures forwards and backward before any field testing would be attempted.

Bright and early on a sunshine-filled Saturday in November, Michael and his family loaded up the new ship and proceeded to the same area where Bill had tested his craft. Michael assured Becky that his intentions for this trial run only consisted of practicing his takeoffs and landings. She reluctantly agreed even though she preferred both his feet securely on the ground.

Michael's heart raced as he climbed into the cockpit preparing for liftoff. The kids jumped up and down with excitement as their daddy lowered the hatch and gave them the thumbs up sign. Michael attempted to play down the situation around his family regarding this test, but deep down he knew anything could go wrong. The mechanics of the craft failing didn't bother him as much as the thought of himself failing, and in essence, eliminating any hope of rescuing Bill. Even though it had been over ten years since he had helped his dad fly their plane, Michael's confidence soared as the adrenaline pumped through his body.

With only one activated panel, the ship shot down the old road. Michael closed his eyes while pulling back on the wheel. The small craft lifted gracefully into the morning sky. Everyone on the ground ecstatically cheered as Michael circled the area. Michael was kind of ecstatic too as a big smile spread across his face. Then came the reality, he had to land the thing! He recalled his father's instructions and training concerning practice landings as the old "touch and go" procedure.

From the ground, it appeared Michael was lining up with the runway and preparing to make his landing. The craft glided toward the strip while his family held their breath in anticipation of a perfect landing. The rear wheels of the ship lightly touched the ground momentarily and then to everyone's surprise, the craft lifted back into the sky! This procedure happened four more times while the family looked on. Finally, on the fifth approach the front wheels also touched down. Becky blew out a heavy sigh as the craft coasted to a stop. They excitedly ran to greet Michael with Becky highly concerned as to what he was doing. He reassured her of his intentions to practice takeoffs and landings, and not to be alarmed.

Meanwhile, Michelle and Marty anxiously pleaded with their dad, "Can we go for a ride? Please, can we Dad? We won't get in the way or say a word!"

Michael looked at Becky knowing she would definitely say no. In his own heart, he remembered the first time his dad took him up. He was only Marty's age at the time, and it created a bond with his father he'd never forgotten. When the kids saw their dad looking at Becky, they immediately surrounded her, each grabbing a leg and still pleading, "Please Mom, just this once. We'll never ask for anything again!"

"I know I may live to regret this," Becky announced, "but I guess it's okay with me." A squeal of joy erupted from the kids. Michael raised his eyebrows shocked by Becky's response. Michelle and Marty raced over to the craft attempting to get in when their mother firmly added, "But only one at a time. If something dreadful is going to happen, I want one of them with me."

"Who's going to be first?" Michael asked cheerfully. Michelle, knowing her little brother could hardly stand the suspense said, "Go ahead Marty. I'll go second." There was no argument from Marty as he scurried up into the Light Assimilator II. Michael smiled and winked at his daughter in approval as he climbed into the craft. Marty had already strapped himself in the rear seat and was ready to go.

"All set copilot?" Michael asked preparing for takeoff. "I'm ready Dad," responded Marty as he dug his fingers into the sides of the seat. "This will be better than the Space Mountain ride at Disneyland they wouldn't let me go on because I was too short!"

"Then hold on, because here we go!" Michael activated a panel and they accelerated down the road into the bright blue sky. Marty didn't say a word, but his eyes stretched a mile high! Michael circled the area coercing Marty to look out the window and wave to his mom and sister. After three loops, Marty's boyish courage enabled him to let loose and wave to the girls. By the time Michael landed the craft, Marty was begging for more. Michael explained how Michelle had courteously allowed her younger brother to go first, and now it was her turn.

Michelle immediately barraged her dad with questions concerning the gadgets in the front of the ship. Her father reminded her she promised to be quiet on this little jaunt. She soberly sat back in her seat adjusting her safety belt. After taking off, Michael smiled back at Michelle. "Okay honey, what questions can I answer for you?" A hundred questions burst forth and Michael tried to explain all of them. Finally, he said, "I'd better set this craft down before your mom starts getting concerned."

With Michelle safely on the ground Michael asked, "Would you like to go for a spin, Becky?"

She graciously declined. "I would just as soon keep both feet safely on the ground."

I need to check one more thing and I'll be right back." Becky didn't have a chance to respond before Michael closed the hatch rocketing down the runway into the morning sky. The three of them watched as Michael circled his family and then, to their utter surprise, the craft suddenly disappeared!

"MICHAEL!" Becky screamed out as she pulled her children in close to her.

Innocently Marty asked, "Is Daddy coming back soon?"

"We hope so," was Becky's quivering reply. She had been intently watching the sky when she glanced down to see Michelle with her eyes closed and her hands folded.

At that moment, Marty yelled out, "I see him!" He pointed to the sky and amidst the deep blue sky appeared the Light Assimilator II. It circled the runway coming in for another three-point landing.

Becky didn't know whether to hug him or hit him as Michael dismounted from the craft. "What do you think you were trying to pull?" Becky yelled as she neared her husband.

Michael took the next five minutes trying to explain the fact that if he had asked her permission to test the time warp, she would have said no. But he had to make sure it worked before proceeding further with the project. At that point, he pulled out next Saturday's paper and announced, "It worked!" as he smiled from ear to ear. Becky finally agreed he probably had to test it, and the discussion ended. The kids were just glad Dad had returned safe and sound.

The series of events transpiring that Saturday morning exceedingly pleased Michael. Somehow, he had constructed a time machine from Bill's blueprints, successfully flown a craft after not flying for ten years, and he had convinced his wife that this undertaking was the right thing to do. Now, all he needed was the propelling device Bill had spoken of in his letter.

The next two days involved researching the small nuclear motor the government introduced the preceding year. Michael discovered one of the main principals initiating the project was Senator Robert Duncan from California. The article listed him as an advisor to the defense chairman. This information brought an idea to mind inspiring Michael to pick up the telephone and attempt to reach the senator.

Even though the senator was residing at his Los Angeles office for the next two weeks, his office informed Michael the senator was busy and would return his call as soon as possible. Michael had heard this standard response before and knew he'd be lucky if he ever received as much as a form letter from the California politician. "If I can get the senator's attention, he may listen to what I have to say," Michael said to himself as he sat down with next Saturday's paper and began reading.

CHAPTER TWENTY-ONE

Two days later, on Thursday morning, the Senator quietly sat reading the morning paper at his home when he was interrupted by his personal secretary, Jim Weisman. "Besides your regular junk mail, you received one interesting letter you may want to examine."

Senator Duncan unfolded the letter that read:

> "Enclosed is the front page of next Saturday's L.A. Times. I have access to the process from which I secured this newspaper. National security could be at stake if this procedure were to fall into the wrong hands. I did consider contacting Congressman Fulcher, but as you can see, the Representative will incur is a broken nose and index finger in a car wreck. Your silence concerning this matter would be appreciated. You may want to wait until Saturday to verify the validity of this paper. Once you are completely satisfied, I would like to talk to you concerning this matter."
>
> "P.S. I will call you at 9:00 A.M. Saturday morning for your response."

This intriguing information aroused the Senator's curiosity. Skeptical as to the validity of the situation, he called his secretary back in the room. "Do we have any idea who this character is?"

His secretary shook his head no. "There was no return address on the envelope, but the postmark indicates a Riverside origination."

"Why don't you give Pete Fulcher's aide a call and see how the representative is doing. If he's okay, I'm not going to get overly concerned about this." Ten minutes later the senator received a message from his secretary confirming Representative Fulcher was alive and well. The senator considered the message from this Michael person a hoax and went back to his newspaper.

Friday evening, when the senator returned home from a political function, he noticed the message light blinking on his answering machine. "This is Jim. On the evening news tonight, they stated that Congressman Pete Fulcher was involved in a two-car mishap on an entrance ramp to Interstate 5. He was not hurt seriously but received treatment for a broken nose and a broken finger. You're not thinking what I'm thinking about that newspaper, are you?"

The senator didn't know what to think. He fumbled through his papers until he located the newspaper and letter he had received from Michael. Studying over the article about the accident, he couldn't find any discrepancies from what had just been reported to him.

At 6:00 A.M. on that cool Saturday morning, the senator rolled out of bed at the first buzz of his alarm. During the night, thoughts concerning the morning paper and what enlightening facts it may bring had created a restless sleep. After grabbing his robe from the back of the bedroom door, he trotted down the circular staircase to the front entrance. For once, the paper boy had been on time and on target. Typically, the senator would be fishing the paper out of the bushes or off the roof. A cellophane bag strapped on by a small rubber band encased the tautly rolled L. A. Times. With the paper clenched tightly in his hand, he hurried back into the house to the study. First he spread out the front page he had received from Michael. Apprehensive of what he may find, he very slowly unrolled the morning paper on the desk. There before him were identical front pages!

"How can this be?" Senator Duncan questioned in disbelief. Sitting down, he carefully checked each article word for word to assure the paper's validity. For two hours, he read and examined the two papers.

Much to his amazement, not as much as a period appeared out of place. Perplexed and stunned, the senator showered, got dressed, grabbed a cup of coffee, and returned to the study to wait for a call he hoped would come.

At exactly 9:00 A.M. he wasn't disappointed. Anxiously he grabbed the phone on the first ring. "Hello, this is Senator Duncan."

The voice on the other end replied, "This is Michael. I hope you appreciated your advance news. Are you interested in pursuing the procedure by which I obtained this futuristic object?"

"Who are you and where are you from?" the senator demanded. "What kind of scam are you running?"

"My identity is not important, and I can guarantee you this is no scam. I have a breakthrough that could literally change the history of the world." Michael knew that statement would get the senator's attention.

Silence momentarily filled the airwaves. "When can you meet me at my office?"

"In order for me to demonstrate this procedure to you, we must meet out in the desert," Michael stated.

"Wait a minute!" the senator interrupted. "If you expect me to meet somebody, who won't tell me their name, out in the desert, you must take me for an idiot!"

"I'm sorry Senator, but I need an open space to demonstrate my findings to you. If you are still interested, meet me at the old station on the north side of Lucerne Valley. It's located 17 miles east of I-15 on Highway 18. Be there at 11:00 A.M. and come alone, or I will deny everything." Michael didn't wait for a response quickly hanging up the phone. He was satisfied the message had not fallen on deaf ears.

At 10:45 A.M. Michael arrived at the old station, promptly unloading the Light Assimilator II. If the senator did double-cross him by bringing in the authorities, this would be his best means of escape. The minutes ticked away until 11:30 flashed on his digital watch. "He must have chickened out," Michael thought as he began loading his craft back on the trailer. The major question now would be, who he could attempt to contact to acquire a nuclear motor. Michael's train of thought was interrupted by the sound of a vehicle coming in his direction. An ominous black Mercury with California plates pulled up next to him. The power window on the driver side slowly descended revealing Senator Duncan driving the car. He appeared to be the only occupant in the vehicle.

"I am Robert Duncan. Are you Michael?" he inquired.

"Michael Hansen," he replied thrusting his hand through the window to greet the senator. "I'm very happy you decided to follow up on my invitation."

"You left me no choice. My curiosity got the best of me. So what is this great marvel of yours?" he inquired as he opened the car door.

Pointing toward the Light Assimilator II Michael stated, "This is the invention my partner Bill Abrams and I have developed. It is a craft that is powered by the radioactive rays of the sun."

"If all you dragged me out here for was to show me a solar powered aircraft, I may as well head back home." The senator slammed his car door in disgust. "I want to know how you did the newspaper switch."

"You wouldn't believe me if I told you," Michael replied. "The best way to convince you will be to show you. Do you have any problem with flying in a small aircraft?"

"You want me to get in that thing with you?" replied the senator angrily gesturing towards the ship. "First you want me to drive out in the middle of the desert and then you want me to go for a flight in that cracker box! I think you'd better find another senator."

Michael calmly suggested, "You know as well as I do, Senator, that whoever provides this kind of breakthrough information to the President could better themselves significantly in the political future."

Senator Duncan, who had turned to get back in the car, froze in his tracks. Turning around he asked, "Can you get me an entire paper, front to back, for a week from now?"

"If you've got a dollar, I can get you to the news stand." A wide smile, reminiscent of Bill's mischievous grin, spread across Michael's face as he motioned the senator over to the Light Assimilator. Michael momentarily turned to open the hatch when he heard the click of the car door behind him. He wheeled around to see a well-dressed man in his 40's step out of the back door of the car.

With both hands, the man pulled up a .45 revolver aimed directly at Michael's head and yelled, "FREEZE MISTER!" Michael froze instantly as his eyes widened staring down the barrel of that handheld cannon. Any attempts to escape in this situation could prove futile or even fatal!

CHAPTER TWENTY-TWO

Immediately, Senator Duncan stepped between Michael and the gunman telling his bodyguard to lower his gun. "This is my personal secretary, Jim Weisman," the senator said apologetically to Michael. "I couldn't risk coming out here by myself in case this was a set up. If it's still okay with you, I'd like to go for that little flight."

Michael heaved a sigh of relief, walked over and introduced himself to Mr. Weisman. The senator and Mr. Weisman proceeded to inspect the craft carefully before the senator consented, climbing in the back seat. Within minutes, Michael and the senator lifted off into the noontime sky. Questions flowed from the senator regarding the energy source for the small craft, but Michael indicated he could not reveal its secret at this time. While the senator carefully examined the ship, Michael activated the remaining light panels. For one brief instant, they shot through time with the computer returning them in the same location seven days later. Not even realizing what had occurred, the senator continued to ask questions concerning the craft. Michael's only response was, "Sit back and prepare to land."

"Land! We just got up here," the senator argued. "We haven't gone anywhere yet." He glanced out the window to find Jim Wiseman, gone. His car was nowhere to be seen, and even Michael's vehicle, vanished. "What is going on here?" he whispered lightly sitting back in his seat while the craft touched down.

Michael coasted the craft along the dusty road to within a quarter of a mile from the old station. As the senator disembarked he asked, "Where are we?"

"The question is not where are we, but when are we? For your information, this is Saturday November 21st." Silence filled the air as the two men covered the remaining distance to the station. Determined to get the facts, Senator Duncan marched through the door of the old dilapidated filling station. Behind the cluttered desk sat an elderly man with his dusty boots up on the desk intently watching a small television. When the two men entered, the old man quickly arose to greet the senator by name.

Still a trifle stunned from the events transpiring before him, the senator didn't respond. "Did you forget my name already senator?" asked the elderly gentleman. "I'm Joe Williams. Remember, I met you last week? I thought it was just us old folks who forgot things like that."

To the best of his recollection, the senator had never met this old man before. He tried to cover himself by stating he remembered him, but right now he had other things on his mind. "Do you have any newspapers available today?"

"Not today," replied Joe. "With the big game going on, we were sold out by 9:00 A.M."

The senator thought for a moment. "Could I write you a check to get a Snickers and some cash? I seem to have run a little short."

"I guess a U.S. Senator should be good for cashing a check," Joe replied as he walked back behind the register. "How much do you need?"

"Twenty should get me by," Senator Duncan said as he bent over to write out the check. "What's today's date, Joe?" he asked slyly as he started writing.

"It's the 21st," Joe replied. "Just a few more days until Turkey Day. Hope you got your bird already with the shortage and all this year."

The senator nodded his head yes while ripping out the check and handed it to Joe. "By the way," he added, "do you happen to know of any other places close we can pick up today's paper?"

Joe thought for a minute scratching his thinning gray hair as he handed him his candy bar. "If you drive back to Victorville you might find one."

As the two prepared to leave, Joe returned to his desk and continued to watch his program. "Quite a ball game on guys. You're welcome to grab a cold one and pull up a chair."

Senator Duncan suddenly became interested in football. "What game do you have on today?"

Joe looked up at the senator like he had to be kidding. "How can anyone live in L.A. and not know who's playing today. The USC – UCLA game is going on at the Rose Bowl. They have the two best records in college football this year. That's all we've heard about this past week and why I'm out of newspapers. A lot of people didn't appreciate the early start time just to appease the T.V. station."

"What's the score?" the senator asked.

"It's 14 all," Joe replied. "but USC is driving and should at least get a field goal before halftime."

Senator Duncan didn't want to embarrass himself anymore. Instead, he said goodbye and turned for the door. The entire time Michael, silently stood in the doorway smiling at the senator's antics. Michael wanted him to draw his own conclusions of what had occurred.

Back at the ship the senator asked, "Can we take a quick trip over the Rose Bowl? A good actor and a football game video could have set up that station scene. But I doubt if you could get the Bruins and the Trojans, and 80,000 people to cooperate with you."

Michael smiled as they took to the sky and banked to the west for the Rose Bowl. From the air, they could see the parking lot overflowing with cars, vans, and buses. As they neared the top of the stadium, Michael handed his binoculars to the senator. Stillness like that in a sanctuary filled the craft as the senator viewed a packed stadium of cheering spectators. The two teams returned to the field as the halftime festivities concluded. There was no denying the Trojans and Bruin's uniforms. The scoreboard gave the halftime tally of USC 17 and UCLA 14.

Michael reluctantly interrupted the senator's bewildered gaze. "We do need to leave this airspace soon before we run into a blimp or something." The senator quietly agreed, and they headed toward the desert.

"Now," Michael took a deep breath as he began his prepared discourse, "this craft can go into the future or back in time indefinitely. We can travel 7 ½ days per second in either direction. The same process could be used for space travel at a speed of 186,000 miles per second. This procedure is a revolutionary process known only to my partner and myself. We are offering this technology to you and the U.S. Government for one small favor."

"Before we get to your favor," the senator jumped in, "let me see you take us back to where we started."

"Your wish is my command," Michael gladly responded programming the computer and activating the remaining light panels. "Don't blink!" Michael announced as the surroundings momentarily blurred for a split second. "Now take a look below us," Michael said as he looked out the window. There, below, stood Jim Weisman and the vehicles they had left earlier.

"Put us down now!" commanded the senator. Once on the ground, the senator immediately asked his aide, "How long have we been up there?"

Somewhat surprised, Weisman looked at his watch. "Less than three minutes. It seemed for a few seconds the ship had disappeared, but then it was there again."

Senator Duncan stared at his watch. According to it, he had been gone for an hour! He looked at Michael, then over to the ship, and back at Michael again. Michael raised his eyebrows and smiled. "I told you so."

Dazed from the incredible events of the last hour, the senator stated, "This desert sun must be getting to me. Let's get something to drink." Getting in the senator's car, the three of them drove to the station and found the old man sitting on the shaded porch in a wooden rocker. Exiting the car, the senator greeted Joe like an old friend. Mr. Williams vaguely recognized Senator Duncan from past campaigns and had to be reminded of his first name. After purchasing three sodas, the senator turned to Michael and admitted, "I think we need to have a private conversation." Michael and Senator Duncan returned to the car while Jim and Joe chatted in the shade of the tattered station.

In the car, the senator asked, "So what's this little favor you and your partner were thinking of, seven or eight figures?"

"It isn't money we're after, Senator. To make a long story short, my partner is trapped back in prehistoric times in a ship like this and needs a lightweight motor to propel him to a time when he can time travel again. The only thing I have discovered suitable for this purpose is the small nuclear engine you helped approve to Congress a year ago."

"No way!" the senator interrupted. "The makeup of that piece of equipment is top secret. There is no possible way we could release the hardware or specifications to a civilian. We can't risk this motor falling into the wrong hands."

"Can you risk my piece of equipment falling into the wrong hands? I would guarantee that as soon as I return, you can have your precious nuclear motor back." Silence filled the car as the senator sat shaking his head no. Michael reasoned further, "You know I could zoom into the future about 50 years and pick this motor up at the local parts store. But I don't want to risk coming out of time warp in some disastrous situation that I couldn't get out of. The future of my friend's existence depends on this motor."

Senator Duncan continued staring at the floor shaking his head. "There isn't any way I could convince the defense department to do it."

Finally, Michael pulled out all stops. "I see you're going to be up for reelection next year. I suppose it takes a lot of money to finance a Senate campaign these days. If a person could only get their hands on a Wall Street Journal a couple weeks in advance, it could make a world of difference in their available resources for a campaign drive." Michael looked over at Senator Duncan. He had stopped shaking his head no and slowly turned to stare silently at Michael.

CHAPTER TWENTY-THREE

Back in 2351 B.C., Bill left the ancient city of Babylon in the distance where he had buried his message to Michael inside his mummified toolbox. Bill remembered from his archeological magazines exactly where they had been excavating during Michael's time. Only a half an hour of sunlight remained as he neared the Mt. Ararat region. Quickly, he needed to find a location to ride out the oncoming flood. The mountains weren't what he had anticipated. The entire range only rose a third of the height of the modern day mountains.

"I assume that during the great pressure thrust upon the earth from the flood, the mountains will rise," Bill reasoned. "Or maybe the changes that occur during the time of Peleg when the land divides, the mountains around the world will be pushed skyward. And then the valleys, like the Dead Sea, will sink into the earth's surface."

Unfortunately for Bill, the lower mountain peaks will allow the waters to reach a flood stage of 20 feet higher than the tallest mountain much easier. It appeared that no mountains in this area were over 4,000 feet high. All Bill could do was find the highest plateau suitable for landing his craft.

Level mountain tops were hard to find. As his note to Michael indicated, Bill was forced to stay in the Ararat region. Otherwise, Michael would have no possible means of finding him. The sun descended rapidly, and so would Bill if he didn't land soon. At last, a relatively high plain appeared a mile to his left. He said a small "Thank You" to the sky circling around to land. A quick pass over the plateau showed no major obstacles. Bill kept the nose off the ground as long as possible allowing the sturdier rear wheels to absorb the shock of the intermittent rocks and crevasses.

As the light of day faded, Bill exited the craft surveying the plateau for future reference. A light covering of soil and grass carpeted the main rock base. The plateau stretched approximately 250 meters slightly downhill with a steep drop off at the far end. Bill pushed the Light Assimilator back as far as he could so the full length of the landing strip would be available in case he had to attempt an emergency takeoff. A sharp descending cliff on the west side forced Bill to anchor the craft down. The oncoming pulverization of the magnetic poles should cause a major shifting in the earth's position. If his ship remained un-tethered, it could easily be thrown off the side of the mountain and him with it. He looped three strong nylon ropes over and around the ship securing them in the rocks behind the craft.

Darkness set in over the Light Assimilator as Bill collapsed in exhaustion in the cocoon of his cockpit. His long adventurous day included behemoth trying to flatten him, discovering Noah's Ark, encountering ancient Babylonians, and finally landing on a mountaintop. There was no time to reminisce as he still had to prepare the inside of the ship for a long duration. Moving the front seat back as far as possible enabled him to stretch out his legs. The seat was also capable of reclining for sleeping purposes. To be safe, Bill bedded down for the night in his ship. Within a matter of moments, he fell fast asleep.

A few hours later, Bill awoke as the comet broke over the horizon. This new light to the nighttime, combined with the usual evening celestial bodies, lit up the surrounding area like two full harvest moons beaming their soft light down upon the earth. The comet looked ready to strike the unsuspecting planet at any moment. But according to the scripture it would wait until the seventh day of Noah and his family being housed inside the Ark, which would be tomorrow.

Halley's Comet came to mind every time Bill thought about that icy monster in the sky. Bill knew Halley's Comet visited the earth every 76.1 years and the last time was a feeble appearance in 1986, while its 1910 showing had been spectacular. Quick calculations told Bill every ten trips of Halley's Comet would amount to 761 years. Subtractions backward from 1910 indicated appearances in 1149 A.D., 388 A.D., 373 B.C., 1134 B.C., and 1895 B.C. From there, Bill calculated another five trips which brought him back to 2275.5 B.C. "One more time," Bill remarked as he tacked on another 76.1 years. The final figure calculated to 2351.6 B.C.

"Well, what do you know!" exclaimed Bill. "This is Halley's Comet! And in another 56 trips to the earth it will have fizzled down to almost nothing." Bill snapped a few last shots of the comet knowing these would be the most dramatic. Despite the presence of the comet and understanding the consequences of its timely arrival, Bill somehow dropped off to sleep.

Morning presented itself with the comet circling like a vulture ready to strike. This opportunity would be Bill's last chance to stretch his legs on dry ground, so he jumped out of the craft to do some calisthenics. Jogging to the end of the 250 meter runway, he inspected the area for any jagged rocks or deep holes that would hinder a future takeoff attempt. The far northern end of the plateau abruptly ended with a steep devastating drop off of 200 meters.

"You'd definitely have to be airborne by the time you reached this point," Bill commented looking over the vast openness.

Suddenly, his eyes were pulled to the sky as the sound of a crashing wave thundered across the heavens. "It's coming!" Bill exclaimed as he frantically tried to turn and run towards the ship. Huge ice particles from the passing comet attracted to the earth's magnetic poles broke through the water belt heading toward the polar regions. Like a balloon bursting, vast quantities of air escaped into the unending vacuum of the universe. A great suction of wind passed over the earth propelling Bill backward to the edge of the rocky cliff. Helpless, Bill desperately attempted to cling to the flat rock surface above him. Within seconds, millions of tons of ice pounded both ends of the planet altering the earth's course and hurtling Bill 20 meters in the air headfirst onto the rocks of the plateau.

Bill regained consciousness as a driving cold rain pelted his saturated body. A deep cut on his forehead profusely bled down into his eyes and mouth. The torrential rains created a blinding wall of water leaving the visibility at zero. Confused and in shock, Bill didn't know which way to go. Out of desperation he began crawling on his hands and knees making certain he didn't creep over the edge to a certain death. The icy rain pounded his already shivering body like a sea of hail. Bill had never prayed before, but he felt this was as good a time as any to begin. "Please give me strength and guidance to make it back to my ship."

The rush of water running down from the upper parts of the mountain suddenly indicated to Bill he was heading in the right direction! Slowly crawling along the saturated plateau inch by inch in the torrential downpour seemed to take an eternity. At any moment, Bill expected to reach his ship or one of the ropes securing it to the cliff. With each passing minute Bill's doubts of finding his craft increased. "It could have been jolted off the cliff with the impact," he reasoned, "or maybe I already crawled passed it." The earth rumbled and shook beneath him as many internal changes began taking place. Time passed as he blindly forced one knee in front of the other along the seemingly endless rocky plateau.

Bill's battered and bruised body didn't want to continue, but somehow he gathered enough strength, inching his way forward until out of total exhaustion, he collapsed in the rain and the mud. The loss of blood from the gash on his head combined with the frustration of not knowing where he was found Bill wishing for death to come quickly. Apparently, this God had answered his prayer with his eternal demise. Sprawling out on the rain-soaked ground, Bill started to bring his arms into his aching body when he brushed against something familiar with his right hand. Stretching out his tired arms, he located the end of one of the nylon ropes he had anchored the ship with! Bill immediately grasped the rope with high expectations of finding his vessel, only to discover a slack line that wasn't holding anything. Apparently, the ship must have broken loose and was jolted over the edge by the comet's impact. Bill collapsed face first in the mud crying bitterly.

But something inside told him to follow the rope. Slowly he edged his way along the limp piece of nylon until he reached a frayed broken end. He tried to look at the severed end hoping it would give him some clue as to what happened. He wanted to cry, but his tears would not flow. Instead, the torrential rain pelting his head and running down his face served as his tears. Saying one last prayer, Bill shielded his eyes and tried to look to the heavens. He couldn't see far, but what he saw appeared to be the faint outline of the tip of his wing only two meters above him! With a new surge of energy, Bill scrambled to his feet clinging to the wing of the Light Assimilator. He said a thousand "Thank yous" as he groped around the ship to the hatch.

"The impact was strong enough to break the ropes, but hadn't thrown the ship over the cliff," Bill said stripping off his saturated robe. He quickly climbed in his craft trying to keep as much moisture out as possible.

Once inside his temporary safe haven, Bill grabbed a warm, dry blanket and immediately wrapped it around his shivering body. The deep cut on his aching head was well cleansed and oozing slightly. The medicine kit provided Neosporin, a couple butterfly strips, and a sterile pad to tape to his aching head. Glancing at the ship's clock, he noticed he'd only been outside for two hours. It seemed more like five or six. Utterly exhausted from what had transpired, Bill drifted off to sleep.

CHAPTER TWENTY-FOUR

Hours later, rumblings and shifting of the earth's surface jolted Bill from his state of hibernation. "This will be a constant occurrence throughout the duration of the flood," Bill reasoned while he stretched for his notebook. Turning to reach behind him, Bill bumped his sore head on the seat reminding him what a pounding headache he had from the ordeal earlier. After retrieving two pain killers from his supplies, Bill opened the hatch slightly, filling his drinking glass with rain water. Within seconds, the glass contained an adequate amount of water in the bottom to swallow the pills. Bill's curiosity led him to taste the water composing the protecting agent for the earth. The water looked to be clear and free of pollutants. One taste revealed it to be sparkling fresh, like that from a cold mountain stream.

"A little food might help out my head situation," Bill commented while digging through his rations. For the time being, an abundance of nourishing fruit surrounded him. After eating, Bill traded his blanket for some regular clothes. Inside the cramped quarters of his tiny craft, Bill struggled getting back in his denim jeans. Besides an assorted array of bumps and bruises, Bill discovered he had aching muscles where he didn't even know he had muscles.

The remainder of the day consisted of filling his notebook with the events marking the first day of the Great Flood. What little semblance of daylight existed, slowly faded into total darkness as the rain continued to pound the outer hull of the small craft. The constant sound of the rain had a hypnotizing effect on the ship's inhabitant. Bill fell asleep wondering what his fate would be.

Day two brought the same pouring rain with no hope of subsiding. Boredom soon set in with nothing to do but eat and read. Bill could readily see that conserving food was going to be a major problem. Rationing would have to be implemented immediately. In the meantime, Bill had to find something extremely interesting to pass the time or he would go crazy.

"This is worse than Chinese water torture," Bill said out loud as he sorted through his books to see what reading material was available. Language books didn't seem to be Bill's idea of exciting reading. Then he spotted Michelle's Bible. In the first few chapters, that little book had provided answers to some of the earth's most mysterious questions. "I wonder what else this book has to say?" Bill queried as he unzipped the white Bible and started "In the beginning..."

Rereading the account of the flood, this time he noted that on the first day of the flood the fountains of the great deep burst forth, then the floodgates of heaven were opened. "The pressure of the ice hitting the poles could have released springs of water under the surface. But it says the fountains of the great deep, which could refer to the oceans. The world had been rotating on its magnetic axis. When the ice hit, it shifted the world to the current axis we have today. That sudden shift would have thrown the oceans over dry ground. This massive tidal wave mowed down all plants and animals in its path creating the vegetation deposits needed to form the billions of tons of coal we have surrounding the earth." A smile came over his face as more pieces of the evolutionary puzzle fell into place.

Days passed as Bill read chapter after chapter and book after book of the historical masterpiece. The chronicle of the history of the world turned into the history of God's chosen people as Bill made his way through the Old Testament.

While examining the plight of Job, Bill came upon something quite interesting contained in the 40th chapter. The 15th verse began, "Look at the behemoth, which I made along with you and which feeds on grass like an ox. What strength he has in his loins, what power in the muscles of his belly! His tail sways like a cedar, the sinews of his thighs are close-knit. His bones are tubes of bronze, his limbs like rods of iron. He ranks first among the works of God."

Kabe had talked about behemoth, and this definition precisely described the beast Bill had a close encounter with earlier in his trip. Noticing the footnote below, Bill noted the Bible suggested behemoth may have been a hippopotamus or an elephant.

"Hogwash!" Bill exclaimed emphatically. "Neither of those eat grass like an ox nor have a tail that sways like a cedar. I imagine the greatest of the works of God would be the largest. And if memory serves me right, fossils have been found of an enormous creature called the Supersaurus measuring over 120 feet long. I think that would certainly qualify as the largest animal on earth."

"Why would the men rewriting the Bible in modern times not consider such a creature to be a dinosaur?" Bill contemplated for a moment as he noted the passage in his notebook. Then he continued to write the following as Bill philosophized, "Many old Bible scholars would not recognize the existence of the extinct dinosaurs because they felt they were anti-scriptural. These full grown beasts could not be contained in a vessel like the ark. They did not consider the possibility of infant dinosaurs making the trip with Noah. So even if this passage perfectly described a dinosaur, the scholars refused to reference them in the Bible."

This occurrence in the Scripture sparked an interesting thought in Bill's mind. This book of Job, located well after the time of the flood in Genesis, talked of a man looking at a behemoth. "That means dinosaurs must have existed for a while after the flood, but the extreme temperature changes were just too much for them." He recalled an article in one of his recent journals about a scientist who had traveled to deepest, darkest Africa. There he befriended a tribe of natives and conversed with them by showing the natives pictures. In his books, they saw an image of a dinosaur and indicated that one lived in the dense valley in the jungle. "I guess in the proper climate with ample amounts of food and cover, it may actually be possible for one of the great reptiles to exist today still."

The potential existence of a dinosaur during modern times brought a current mythical legend to mind. The story of the Loch Ness monster popped into Bill's thought patterns. For years, the tale of a great sea serpent being sighted in the lake in Scotland had surfaced. Due to the extremely miry condition of the lake measuring over 23 miles long and deeper than parts of the Atlantic, it has been utterly impossible to view the creature under the surface. Some people suggested this sea creature may be a remnant of the dinosaurian age. But skeptics note the fact that the dinosaurs became extinct millions of years previously. There was no possible way a few of them could have survived this long after their ancestor's demise. But now, we may have to consider their disappearance from the earth as only a few thousand years ago. That may put a whole new outlook on the possibility of their existence today!

Bill's writing quickened as he hurried to jot all of his thoughts and theories down on paper. His enthusiasm for life increased as he sensed a feeling of pride knowing he may be on the verge of answering one of history's greatest mysteries. When he completed his writing, he continued his reading of Job in the 41st chapter. It included another passage of scripture that greatly intrigued him.

"Can you pull in the Leviathan with a fishhook or tie down his tongue with a rope?" The chapter went on to say, "Neither hooks, harpoons, or fishing spears can harm him. Any hope of subduing him is false, and the mere sight of him is overpowering. No one is fierce enough to rouse him. Who can strip off his outer coat? Who dares open the doors of his mouth, ringed about with his fearsome teeth? His back has rows of shields tightly sealed together; each is so close to the next that no air can pass between. They are joined fast to one another; they cling together and cannot be parted. His sneezing throws out flashes of light, his eyes are like the rays of dawn. Firebrands stream from his mouth and sparks of fire shoot out. Smoke pours from his nostrils as from a boiling pot over a fire of reeds. His breath sets coals ablaze, and flames dart from his mouth. Strength resides in his neck and dismay goes before him. His chest is as hard as rock, hard as a lower millstone. The sword that reaches him has no effect, nor does the spear or the dart or the javelin. He makes the depths churn like a boiling caldron and stirs up the sea like a pot of ointment. Behind him he leaves a glistening wake, one would think the deep had white hair. Nothing on earth is his equal - a creature without fear. He looks down on all that are haughty. He is king over all that are proud."

Here was the description of a fire-breathing sea serpent that God had created. Bill recalled many legends from the past speaking of a great fire-breathing sea monster attacking and sinking many vessels. The most prevalent example came from the Viking heritage. The Norsemen were so convinced that such a creature existed, they carved the head of a serpent on the bow of their ships. They believed if a monster rose up from the deep, he may be frightened away by the sight of another serpent.

The thought of God creating such a destructive creature somewhat dampened his view of the entire scripture being accurate. After the book of Job, Bill began the Psalms of David. Oddly enough, Bill found two references to Leviathan in the 74th and 104th chapters of this poetic book.

"If more than one author in the Bible verifies the existence of this creature, there may be some validity to their stories. Is it possible this thing actually lived in our oceans, and if so, where is he today?" Bill pondered as he continued his reading.

The next day, Bill began his reading in Isaiah. When he got to chapter 27, verse one stated, "In that day, the Lord will punish with his sword, his fierce great and powerful sword, Leviathan the gliding serpent, Leviathan the coiling serpent. He will slay the monster of the sea."

Bill reflected on that passage for an instant. "I guess that explains what happened to Leviathan, the great sea serpent. One can only imagine why God would have created him in the first place. The only thing Leviathan accomplished was prohibiting people from traveling the oceans. And maybe that's exactly what he wanted!" Bill profoundly exclaimed. "Up until that time, He wanted man to stay put. Then, in His unparalleled wisdom, He decided it was time for man to sail the open seas!"

In a total of fourteen days, Bill completed the Old Testament with a greater understanding of its history and his ancestors. Bill's body longed for activity. Fifteen days of being confined to the small area of the craft wore on Bill's sanity. A couple weeks of confinement began to take its toll on Bill's scent glands, also. He didn't know which was worse; the smell of overripe fruit, the odor of his filled-to-the-rim porta-potty, or the stench of himself!

Suddenly a smile spread across Bill's face. "I can take a shower anytime I want to!" He quickly disrobed for his encounter with the great outdoors. Flipping the latch, he slipped out of the ship onto the ground below. The cold rain immediately drenched Bill's body. The soil covering the plateau had been washed away leaving a smooth rocky surface. Rubbing his body vigorously Bill thought, "I could use a good bar of soap."

To exercise his stiff and inactive muscles, he jumped up and down, and ran in place. The rain didn't feel quite as cold as long as he kept moving. He made certain he stayed within visible distance of his nesting place. Bill could see through the rain about three meters now in comparison to only one or two at the beginning of the flood. He couldn't tell if it was due to less rain or more light. For his future takeoff prospects, he hoped it was the latter of the two.

Limbered-up and refreshed, Bill cleaned out his porta-potty, and climbed back in his little cocoon. Safe and warm in his ship, Bill felt revived from his excursion outside. "I'll have to do this in a couple more days," he reasoned as he fought to clothe himself in the confines of the ship.

The days continued to pass as Bill made his way through the New Testament. His reading marked his first experience with this portion of the scripture. As a Jewish descendant, he was never exposed to the teachings of Jesus. He found it to be entirely different from the Old Testament which dealt with history and the Children of Israel. The New Testament directed itself to all people on earth and showed how God's plan came together by sending His only Son to the earth. So much of the Old Testament pointed to this historic event. Man's hope of salvation unfolded before his very eyes.

"Why haven't I seen this before?" Bill asked himself. Then the reason dawned on him as he started writing in his notebook.

"As an archeologist and a scientist, I believed in the evolution of the species, as ridiculous as it seemed. There is no way an all-powerful God could exist to create the world. Besides, science has supposedly proven this world to be millions of years old, not a few thousand as the Bible indicates. That alone told me the scripture's account of creation as incorrect. And if the beginning of the Bible is wrong, this constitutes the remainder to be false also. Consequently, I did not believe in any of the Bible since I was certain its record of early history was inaccurate. I consider myself an atheist and never did explore the teachings of the New Testament. Little did I know, the earth previously existed in an entirely different environment. That fact threw all of our dating methods out of proportion. The world has been led astray by men toting statistics that are not true. I now know for a fact how the world developed and how the Bible chronicles those exact events. For this reason, I must also believe the remainder of the scriptures. God didn't want to force people to follow him, so he gave them a choice. To show the people how much he really cared, he sent His only son to the people to tell them of his love and concern. Then to show the supreme sacrifice, Jesus gave up his physical life on a cruel cross. The rest is up to man to believe what is written down before him."

A tear trickled down Bill's cheek as he closed the notebook. At that moment, Bill knew the whole truth as he cried out, "Oh God, I am such a sinner. I believe in you and your Son. From now on I am going to make sure everyone I come in contact with knows that too. With the proof I have obtained, I can surely convince thousands of others to change their minds. Please, if it is your will, let me return to my people, in my time, so I can pass this good news on to them."

"You have shown me the light."

CHAPTER TWENTY-FIVE

Bill's calendar read September 16th, marking the 24th day of the Great Flood, and time for Bill to take another invigorating shower. Every two days since his first bathing experience, Bill stepped out in the rain to freshen up. Visibility increased to 10 meters allowing Bill more room to maneuver around the outside of the ship. While jogging laps around the craft, his greatest fear became a reality. Through the constant patter of the pouring rain beating on the rocky surface around him, the faint sound of waves pounding the mountainside below rang loud in Bill's ears. Down on his hands and knees he inched to the treacherous cliff. Lying on his stomach, he peered over the edge into the darkness. The sound of the waves resounded in the distance below, but nothing could be seen through the constant showering of rain from the heavens.

Each day thereafter, Bill ventured out in the pouring rain looking over the cliff. On day 27, the inevitable occurred. The whitecaps of the rising waves faintly presented themselves through the falling rain. According to Bill's approximations, they were 40 meters below him. Day 28 brought the waves 30 meters from the top of the cliff, and day 29 they appeared another ten meters closer. Time was running out for Bill, and he knew his only choice was to attempt a takeoff.

Watching the massive waves crash into the hillside, Bill couldn't help but think back to his higher education and the formation of the fossil record. He had been taught the development of the fossil record on the ocean floor had been a gradual process taking millions of years. According to the fossil record, small sea life would fossilize first, then fish, amphibians, reptiles, and lastly mammals, with each inch of strata taking millions of years to form. This catastrophic event would explain the thousands of exceptions where modern reptiles have been found down in the small sea life level or extinct fish up with the mammals. This catastrophic event also answered the question why the very first inch of strata contains 75% of the evolutionary process. Bill had learned in college that millions of years of evolution occurred on the earth before even one inch of fossils were laid down. But the formation of the fossil record was supposed to be a gradual ongoing process. Those two scientific statements were grave contradictions.

Bill remembered Michael schooling him prior to leaving. "Scientists used to say a fish would die and settle to the bottom of the ocean floor. Over the years, the fish would be covered up with sediment and fossilization would begin from the weight of the dirt and water. You know as well as I do what happens when a fish dies today; another fish comes along and eats it, or it simply decays. Plants and animals are fossilized today by being overlaid in sediment all at once. In most cases, they are buried alive. If something catastrophic happened to the modern world, what would the fossil record in the ocean show?"

Bill never had a chance to respond as Michael enthusiastically continued his presentation. "Naturally, what lives on the bottom of the ocean floor would get covered up first. Next would be fish, and then amphibians living on land adjacent to the ocean. Basically, all that remains would be reptiles and mammals. And consider this: when a reptile dies, it sinks, and when a mammal dies, it floats. I think you can easily see which one is going to show up in the fossil record first."

Bill watched as the waves continued their pounding of the hillside. Then he realized that there would be no shoreline to stop the waves in a few days. The moon's gravitation would create one enormous tidal wave running the width of the planet. Then 12 hours later, with the moon on the other side of the world, the waves would be running the opposite direction. That is why today we find an inch of strata angling to the east and then an inch of strata angling to the west. Science theorized each inch of fossilized strata may have taken a million years to form, when in reality it only took 12 hours! Bill hurried back to the ship to get his findings down on paper.

Day 30 brought the waves so close to the top of the cliff Bill could hear them from within his craft. Outside the ship, visibility increased to 40 meters. Bill carefully walked the length 'of the plateau checking for any jagged rocks that had rolled down the hillside during the deluge or deep ditches cut by the onslaught of water. The make-shift runway seemed to be free and clear of any obstructions.

Bill prepared to leave the plateau at first light of day 31. If his craft could fly on the amount of ultraviolet rays penetrating the remainder of the water belt, he might be able to ride out the last nine days of the flood until the water belt fully dissipated. Only then would Bill be free to zip back to the future.

Bill tossed and turned most of the night. The thought of what tomorrow could bring combined with the sound of the waves smashing nearby created a churning knot deep inside his stomach. The morning brought waves crashing over the top of the lower section of the cliff. To lighten the load, Bill threw out everything not absolutely necessary for his trip home. The time had arrived to face the reality that Michael would not be back to rescue him.

"Even if Michael was able to get back to this time, there would be no possible way he could locate me in this deluge. It would be like trying to find a needle in a haystack," Bill reasoned.

He recorded one final entry in his log noting the time at 10:00 A.M. on September 23, 2351 B.C. as the rising flood waters splashed over the top of the cliff onto the rocky plateau. It was now or never for the hopeful time traveler and his craft. Looking to the heavens, Bill pleaded, "Please, Let There Be Light." He activated every panel on the Light Assimilator. The ship slowly began rolling across the plateau as its only passenger cheered, "Go baby Go!"

Through the water and the rain, the little craft gradually picked up speed. Bill knew that once he passed the halfway point there would be no stopping. As he neared that point, he knew he needed more speed to get airborne, but this would be his only chance. With great anticipation, he raced past the point of no return. The pouring rain hampered Bill's vision, but he knew he would be running out of runway very soon. His speed approached the velocity required to take off when he detected the end of the line 20 meters in front of him. With one last prayer, he pulled back on the wheel at the edge of the cliff. Straight off the plateau the ship barely flew a few feet above the rising waters.

Closing his eyes Bill said a big "Thank You" only to open them and find the crest of a two meter wave coming right at him! Bill tried to attain more altitude, but there wasn't enough time. The forceful wave crashed into the landing gear of the craft sending the nose of the helpless ship down in the violent waters of the deep. Quickly responding, Bill had no choice but to abandon ship. Opening the hatch, the flood waters rushed in the sinking craft as Bill swam out and away from his submerging vessel. He turned, painstakingly watching his Light Assimilator and his only hope for the future slowly disappear into the miry depths of the rising flood. Down with it went his photography equipment, his notes, his food, and any hope of survival. Bill wanted to sink with his ship and get it over with, but his natural instinct found him swimming with the waves back to the plateau he had just left.

Grabbing the ridge and pulling himself up, he saw something astonishing! "I must be hallucinating," Bill said as he froze dumbfounded. There, not more than 10 meters in front of him, sat his Light Assimilator! Scrambling up the slippery rocks, Bill hurried over to this ship sent from heaven. "This couldn't have washed up on shore!" Bill exclaimed as he ran over to the hatch and opened it.

Inside, much to his surprise, sat Michael at the controls! "Get in!" Michael yelled. "I thought I had lost you for sure."

Stunned from what had just transpired, Bill was at a loss for words standing in the pouring rain staring up at Michael. After a momentary lapse, Bill responded to Michael's outstretched arm climbing into the back seat of this new craft. "My ship is out there," Bill said still dazed from his crash. "We've got to get my ship back!"

"We've got to get out of here," responded Michael anxiously. "The rising water will completely flood this plateau any minute, and then both of us will be history! Are you all strapped in?"

Snapping the shoulder harness securely in place, Bill announced, "Ready." Hearing that response, Michael punched the light panel controls. They were taxiing the strip much too slowly when Bill said in a concerned voice, "You can't take off at this speed. I already tried it." At that moment, Michael pushed another button that thrust Bill back in his seat while the Light Assimilator II shot down the watery plateau and up into the rain filled sky.

"All right!" Bill exclaimed. "What do you have under the hood of this thing?"

"Just what the expert prescribed," quipped Michael. "One of those new-fangled nuclear motors fit right in here. I didn't have to change the craft size a bit. It only added 700 pounds to the total structure."

"Well, how on earth could you possibly find me in all this pouring rain?" Bill inquired as he looked around to see if there were any other changes in his original design.

"There was one other improvement I made to your plans. Your message said you were trapped in the Great Flood. I remembered my Bible stories enough to know it rained for 40 days and 40 nights. I naturally expected to search for you through the pouring rain, so I installed a radar device. What I wasn't anticipating was your light panels reflecting the radar. I've been scanning this area for two days, and I didn't see a thing until your ship moved! Then it was too late for me to catch up with you."

"So, where to now captain?" Bill asked jokingly.

Michael thought for a moment. "If the 40 days and nights prediction is correct, we'd better follow the sun around the earth for the next nine days. That way, if this government product would happen to fail us along the way, we may have enough light available to keep us aloft."

A momentary hush fell over the craft as Bill put his hand on Michael's shoulder and said in a soft, sincere voice, "Thanks, friend." Both men choked up for a minute until Bill added, "You're the second friend that saved my skin this trip."

"What are you talking about?" inquired Michael.

Bill then began his story about Kabe and King Pepi II. The next nine days were spent telling stories, eating what food supplies Michael had brought, and watching the pouring rain as the Light Assimilator II circled the saturated earth. Together, they patiently waited for the flood of rain to stop falling from the heavens. Each day the skies lightened until the morning of the 41st day and the rains ended. Above shone a bright yellow sun unhampered by a water belt. Below stretched an enormous ball of water unhindered by shores or mountains. With plenty of ultraviolet rays available to power the ship Michael shut down the nuclear motor.

They were currently over North America and could see the newly formed ice cap arching down through Iowa. The unhindered waves circling the globe crashed into this new shoreline crushing seashells and other crustaceans. This action would create many limestone quarries near ground level in the Midwest region.

A year later, as the flood waters retreated, a river of ice would flow down the Missouri River basin. The strong winds blowing from the west would pick up the sedimentary dust from Nebraska and Kansas. The river of ice would act like a snow fence depositing the dust in drifts on the east side of the ice flow. These would become the Loess Hills, or windblown hills, stretching from Northern Iowa to Northern Missouri. These are the only known windblown hills in North America.

So many questions were being answered, but the time had come. "Ready to zip back home?" Michael asked expecting a positive response.

"Could we circle the area where you picked me up before we take off?" Bill asked.

Michael considered that an odd request, but agreed. Checking his latitude and longitude readings, he programmed in the course. "If you're expecting to find your ship floating on the water, don't get your hopes up."

As they neared the location, Michael looked out the window and astonishingly exclaimed, "What in the world is that!"

With his patented smile on his face, Bill replied, "That's what I wanted you to see. Isn't it fantastic?"

"Are you trying to tell me that is Noah's Ark!" Michael exclaimed still not believing his own eyes. "That thing is enormous! It would put a cruise ship to shame. How could a man back in this day and age possibly build anything like that?"

Bill thought for a second. "With three dedicated sons and a little heavenly advice." They both chuckled at that. Then Bill asked, "Did you happen to bring a camera with you?"

Michael regretfully shook his head no. "I was in such a hurry once the government gave me permission to leave, I took off before they changed their mind."

"And to think I had the whole thing on film," Bill said disgustingly. "Oh well, I can always come back with this ship once I get rested up and restocked."

"I don't know," Michael added cautiously. "The government was pretty demanding about wanting this motor back right away."

"We can easily avoid them," Bill interrupted. "I'll just leave you off with your family, pick up what I need, and will be gone in a flash."

Michael didn't respond immediately. Then very softly he said, "We can't avoid the government. They've got Becky and the kids." Michael emotionally broke down as he forced out the words.

Bill's mouth dropped open in shock. "They did what!"

Michael tried to regain his composure. "To make sure I would bring this motor back immediately, they took my wife and family into custody until I return. I made a deal with Senator Duncan to provide me with the motor if I'd get him a future Wall Street Journal. He provided the motor all right, but added a new set of rules to the game when he delivered it. I'm sorry, but I can't take the chance of you going anywhere with it once we get back."

"I understand completely," Bill regretfully replied. "Under those circumstances, I'm surprised Becky even let you come."

"Once they told me the conditions I wasn't going to do it, but Becky insisted I try to get back here and rescue you," Michael admitted.

Bill smiled. "Remind me when we get back to give that lady a big hug and a kiss. And make sure I buy Michelle a new Bible. Unfortunately, it went down with the ship. I would have never made it through the past 30 days without it."

After one more look at the Ark, Bill remarked, "Let's get out of here. Even without the nuclear motor I can still come back this far sometime in the future."

Michael didn't respond to that statement but instead asked, "Where shall we go from here? I don't know about you, but after riding around in this thing for the last eleven days, I could go for a little leg action and a good night's sleep."

"I know just the place. There's a tranquil haven south of L.A. about 100 years from now that will suit you perfectly."

Within 90 minutes, they arrived at a peaceful time in the earth's history when the land appeared fresh and new. Michael gazed at the landscape, impressed with how the L.A. area used to look. After a restful night's sleep, Bill took the helm and guided Michael on a little sightseeing tour of the planet earth in the year 2240 B.C. Michael had the opportunity to view the newly formed Grand Canyon. As flood water drained down the Colorado River basin, it was backed up by a land bridge at the southwest end of where the Grand Canyon eventually would be. Two great lakes appeared spanning up into the Colorado region. Eventually, the land bridge would burst from all the water pressure behind it. In a matter of days, billions of gallons of water would rush through the canyon area cutting a gorge over a mile deep in the freshly laid soil exposing layers and layers of sediment.

He witnessed the continents still joined together into one huge land mass just as he had theorized. The youthful Sahara Desert began showing forms of barrenness while the wildlife surrounding the Nile River basin frolicked in the sun. The pyramids looked spectacular in their full limestone casing with the head of the newly buried Sphinx guarding the shrines. And man remained centrally located in the Middle East region waiting to be divided by God's ominous insight and power. The earth presented itself so fresh and pure. Both men found themselves wishing man had not been given the capabilities of spoiling the paradise God had provided.

For their return trip home, they agreed that no human confrontations should be attempted. The stakes were too high considering the state of Michael's family. Michael's primary concern now fell on getting back to Becky and the kids. Bill computed a direct flight back home without any stops. "What date did you leave?" Bill asked as he ran computations on the computer.

"December 13th," Michael responded. "I suppose you have to make sure we don't get back before I left."

"I don't want to put you in double jeopardy," Bill said jokingly. "But I would like to get back before Christmas. It's going to be a very special Christmas this year. For once in my life, I can realize the true meaning of this sacred holiday."

With a flip of the switch, the two of them began their journey. Back to a time when crime desecrated the country; one-third of the world's population went to bed hungry; pollution filled the land, water, and air; and most people were only concerned about one thing, themselves.

CHAPTER TWENTY-SIX

Once they had bolted into light speed, Michael inquired, "Since I may never get back to the era before the flood, could you explain to me what the conditions of the earth were like?"

Without hesitation, Bill eagerly related this rendition to his friend. "Try to imagine the land masses completely covered with trees, forests and underbrush teeming with the giant creatures of the earth. Visualize, if you can, great dinosaurs munching on the tender leaves from the tops of the tall trees. Man, for his own protection, cleared away massive amounts of timber to impede the progress of the great beasts. Rivers and streams flowed across the land everywhere. The ever present water belt gave a dark blue hue to the horizon and the skyline. It also kept the temperature constant ranging from 60 to 80 degrees year-round, worldwide. The high humidity constantly weighed upon you. Large amounts of dew collected on the trees and grass each night providing all the moisture needed to thrive."

"The canopy of water also created an atmosphere of hyperbolic oxygen and carbon dioxide. In modern times, we normally have 21% of oxygen in our air. In these conditions, it was closer to 37%. Many of our major sports teams use hyperbolic chambers to heal their athletes on a much faster pace. And the hyperbolic carbon dioxide would make plants grow at an accelerated rate. Do you remember the Jurassic Park movie when they supposedly found mosquitoes trapped in amber with dinosaur DNA contained inside? In reality, the amber had air bubbles with oxygen levels near 37%!" Bill was on a roll.

"Deserts did not exist, only areas of lush green grass. The mountains, as you witnessed, were virtually nonexistent. A 4,000 foot peak may have been the highest elevation in the world easily enabling the flood to cover everything. In modern times, the scientists reason there was no way flood waters could have covered the 29,000 foot peak of Mt. Everest. They do not consider the fact that the mountains may have only been a fraction of the size during the flood. Scientists do not take into consideration their dating methods may be inaccurate due to the different environment caused by a water belt."

Bill continued using his hands to show the actions. "Particles from the comet, attracted to the magnetic poles of the earth, broke through the protective water barrier clamping down on the ends of the unsuspecting planet. Massive chunks of ice pulverized the earth as far south as Iowa creating indentations for the northern lakes region to form. This great pressure burst forth volcanoes and fountains of water from deep inside the earth creating more water to fuel the flood. This tremendous jolt threw the world out of its circular orbit to an oblong rotation around the sun. It also tilted the earth to its new axis throwing the existing oceans out of their beds over the dry land flattening all obstacles in its path. The onslaught of water and debris immediately covered many living plants and animals. The collection of fallen plant life combined with the extreme weight and pressure of the water easily formed the coal deposits we have today. Great masses of dinosaur carcasses pooled together in different locations around the world. Since reptiles do not float when they die, they sank to the depths of the flood waters. They were covered with wave after wave of sediment. The oil from these greasy reptiles collectively seeped into the ground creating today's oil and gas deposits."

Michael was beginning to wonder if Bill was ever going to come up for air.

"The people before the flood were exceptionally tall and strong due to the ideal living conditions. All the people appeared light skinned due to the lack of the sun's damaging rays. They lived to be 900 years old producing large families and many descendants. After the flood, due to the influx of ultraviolet rays, man's life span shortened quickly. Again, man began to populate the world. God saw a need to scatter the people to all corners of the earth, so he confused their languages at the Tower of Babel. The people divided into groups speaking the same dialect. Those people and their herds spread throughout the earth. Soon after, during the time of Peleg, the land masses divided separating the continents. During this separation, many internal changes occurred; the major mountain ranges shot skyward while valleys formed and dropped."

"That explains why some animals are only found in certain areas of the world," Michael interrupted. "But how does that explain the differences we have in the human race today?"

"I have given that much consideration over the past 40 days," Bill reasoned. "And I have come up with the following conclusion. Man, much like animals, can alter their physical traits if they are constantly exposed to one environment. Animals living in colder regions often grow thicker fur and an extra layer of fat to survive in these conditions. Also, a steady diet of certain foods can cause chemical reactions in certain creatures. For instance, do you know why a bald eagle has a yellow beak and legs?"

Michael shook his head having no idea what Bill was implying.

Bill quickly continued, "Bald eagles are born with a white beak and legs. After a steady diet of fish and waterfowl for three or four years, the beak and legs turn yellow when the birds reach maturity. Fish, especially northern pike, have a strong concentration of beta carotene in the meat directly under the skin. The carotene gives it a yellowish tinge. The same applies for the fatty parts of fowl. The concentration of carotene creates the yellow color. The eagles ingest massive doses of carotene day after day after day eventually turning the susceptible parts of their anatomy yellow. This ingestion of carotene has occurred for so many generations in the species, it is now a hereditary trait."

"This metamorphosis could also occur in humans," Bill explained. "Exposure to certain conditions and diets for generations of people could result in a permanent characteristic trait. There are two races of people on the earth today we associate with historically being fish and fowl eaters."

Bill paused a moment awaiting Michael's response. "The Far East Asians and the Eskimos!" Michael proclaimed.

"Correct!" Bill happily announced like a teacher rewarding a student for a good answer. "And what are the major physical characteristics of these people?"

"Both are normally short with a yellowish tint to their skin."

"Right again," Bill positively stated. "A few thousand years dominated by a steady diet of fish and fowl created a permanent physical trait for their descendants. Marriages between family members were a common practice in the early days. We know today that can cause many changes in the genes. Features such as shortness, slant eyes, dark hair, curly hair, whatever, could have become a dominant factor and spread throughout the area. Today we cannot readily see these changes occurring. People today are too mobile. They have a varied diet, and they do not intermarry. Look at the Scandinavians from the northern regions of Europe. They have a light complexion with blond hair. Compare them with the people whose ancestors lived in the hottest portions of the earth. Those regularly exposed to the sun developed a darker skin to protect themselves. Those in between, like the Native Americans, developed a reddish skin. The Eskimos have a much higher fat content than the rest of the world's population to protect themselves from the cold. Just like the animals God has created, man can also adapt to his environment."

"Selective breeding produced many of the physical differences we see today. Tall people were attracted to other tall people. The strong took only the best women for their wives, while the small and weak chose from those remaining. We only have to look as far back as the 1800's in the United States during the slave years to witness a good example. The slave masters tried to pair their strongest men with their sturdiest women producing the best offspring. In less than 100 years of selective breeding, a somewhat physically superior race of people was developed. Hitler's ultimate goal was to do the same with his people. The Jews, living in Germany at that time, were in his mind physically inferior. He planned to eliminate them along with all those who were physically or mentally handicapped. He wanted to create a superior race of blue-eyed blonds. Numerous examples throughout history have resulted in many of the differences we see in the human race today."

"We do the same with our livestock," Bill continued. "We keep only the strongest animals for our breeding stock. New strains are constantly developed. Noah only had one breed of cattle on the Ark. Over the years, man went to different environments and kept only the best stock in their reproductive lines. Many different breeds would be created by man's intervention. While animals, left to their own natural instincts, do not selectively breed. For an example, let's say we take 100 pairs of different purebred cattle and place them on a deserted tropical island with adequate food and water available. If we time traveled to the island 300 years later, what would we find?"

Michael mulled that one over for a moment and facetiously replied, "A whole bunch of cows."

Bill, somewhat disgusted at Michael's response added, "Yes, we'll have a whole bunch of cows. But out of the 100 different breeds, will 200 different breeds have developed?"

"No. They should be pretty much the same," Michael replied.

"Very good," resounded Bill mockingly. "We'd probably end up with a couple thousand medium size brown and black and white face calves, your basic 'Heinz 57' of the cattle variety. Evolutionists say different breeds and even species developed through selective breeding before man appeared on the earth. But without the intervention of man, selective breeding is virtually impossible."

"God gave man dominion over the land and the animals," Bill reasoned. "With that power came responsibility. It is not hard to see how we misused that privilege. Today we are fighting to reintroduce species to areas where they once flourished. Water quality has decreased to undrinkable standards in many parts of the world. Our land has been desecrated by strip miners, loggers, and urban development, while our air grows darker by the day. We are on the verge of using up every natural resource God has provided for us. I have a funny feeling, when this earth is completely depleted and man has squeezed the last ounce of resources out of her; God will put an end to this world as we know it," Bill concluded.

"You sound like you actually believe all this scriptural stuff," Michael responded.

"I have to, Michael," Bill said. "I had the privilege of having the puzzle put together before my very eyes. I know the beginning of the Bible is the honest truth. That realization has given me the faith to believe the predictions and accounts of the future as valid. Did you know that one-fourth of the Bible pertains to things that have not occurred yet and the end of the world?"

Michael shook his head no, overwhelmed by Bill's commitment and enthusiasm. The discussion continued for quite some time as the duo rocketed through time.

CHAPTER TWENTY-SEVEN

The years streaked by as Bill and Michael raced toward home. With two full days of time travel behind them, the pair exited light speed the morning of December 15th. The instruments indicated their location as 165 degrees west. A short jaunt past Hawaii and they would have succeeded in returning home safely.

"Think we'll have a welcoming committee?" Bill asked jokingly.

Surprisingly Michael answered, "We might."

As they passed the crest of the last range of hills between them and their landing area, Bill could see Michael's assumption was correct. Two ominous looking black sedans and the trailer for the Light Assimilator II sat next to the landing strip. Four men decked out in navy blue pinstripe suits and sunglasses immediately surrounded the craft as it coasted to a stop. Mr. Blackman introduced himself as being in charge of this project and indicated they were to go with him.

"What about our craft?" Bill asked arguably.

"My men will see that it is handled properly," Blackman stated factually. "Now if you will please get in the car, we will be on our way."

Bill hopelessly looked at Michael as Blackman opened the back door of the car and motioned for them to get in. Despairingly, he took one final gaze at the Light Assimilator II and despondently followed Michael into the back seat.

In the car, Michael asked questions concerning his family and their destination. Blackman sternly stared straight ahead refusing to acknowledge any of their questions. The car led them to the federal building in downtown Los Angeles. Walking down the long crowded hallway, Bill and Michael could only guess what would happen next. They had committed no crimes or done anything against the United States Government. In turn, they had discovered the foremost scientific breakthrough of the century.

The two men were led into a 12' x 16' dingy gray room. No windows or openings embellished their drab confines, while the lone door provided the only means of escape. The door slammed and locked behind them leaving Bill and Michael alone. The only contents of the room consisted of a 3' x 8' meeting table and three folding chairs. Bill turned to Michael with a bewildered look on his face. "What's going on here?"

Michael shook his head not knowing. "All I know is Senator Duncan said he would have to consider the ramifications of this new invention while I returned to get you. Apparently we're going to discover what his great idea is. I have a funny feeling we're going to come out on the short end of this stick." Michael walked over to one of the chairs and dejectedly sat down.

Two agonizing hours passed before they heard the noise of a key unlocking the door. In walked two men; Mr. Blackman and one other gentleman in uniform. "This is Colonel Stone," Blackman announced to Bill and Michael. "Please be seated," Blackman said, pointing to the chairs behind the table. They adjusted their seats while the colonel pulled up the chair on the near side of the table. Mr. Blackman took a standing position by the door. Michael couldn't tell if Blackman was guarding the door to keep them from escaping or to prevent others from entering.

Stone's ice cold stare pierced Bill and Michael. "Where did you obtain the plans for your vessel?" he demanded.

Before Bill even had a chance to respond, Michael stood up and announced, "We are not going to answer any of your questions until I am allowed to see my wife and my two children!"

Bill was shocked at his partner's forcefulness. Michael had always been the quiet, conservative one, not one to stand up to someone in authority. There was no doubt in Bill's mind of Michael's conviction about this matter.

The colonel insisted, "All we need are a few answers."

"NO!" Michael profoundly stated, folded his arms, and dropped down in his chair. The colonel turned his eyes to Bill.

Bill sat back in his chair raising his eyebrows, "I'm with him. Whatever he says goes." Bill followed his response with a big smile which didn't set well with Stone.

Michael gave Bill a look of thanks as the colonel got up to confer with Blackman. Mr. Blackman momentarily left the room and returned, quietly speaking to Stone. Returning to the table, Stone commented, "I don't know how easy it will be to reunite you with your family, but we will do our best. It may help the procedure if you could answer..."

Michael shut him off right there pounding his fist on the table with a resounding, "No questions!" After a moment of silence, Michael added, "What can you do? Take us out and eliminate us? Not likely in this country."

"That's the kind of attitude we like to hear from our citizens," Stone stated confidently. "We like our people to think that the good old U. S. of A. would never do anything underhanded. It keeps the natives from getting restless. Let me tell you right now, mister, as far as your wife knows, you have not returned. Maybe you will never return having fallen victim of an unforeseen accident. Maybe the rest of your family will be part of some terrible tragedy. People unexplainably disappear from this country all the time with no trace of where they went."

The colonel stared eye to eye with Michael for what seemed to be an eternity. Sitting back in his chair, Stone crossed his arms, took a deep breath, and staunchly rose heading towards the door. Reaching the entrance he yelled, "Guards!" The door immediately unlocked with two towering guards standing at attention. "Take these two men to chamber fourteen on level six."

Dozens of torture devices entered both men's minds as they descended on the elevator below ground level. A long empty hallway brought them to a single door. The lead guard unlocked the door pushing it open to reveal the best thing either man had seen in a long time. Becky, Michelle with a green pocket Bible in hand, and Marty came streaming out of the room to wrap themselves around Michael.

Kisses and tears abounded as the happy family greeted each other. Breaking the little family circle, Michelle grabbed Bill's hand pulling him in. Becky, now realizing Bill's presence, threw her arms around his neck giving him a welcoming squeeze.

Bill returned the hug and gave her a friendly kiss on the cheek. "Thanks," he emotionally said with a crack in his voice. "If it hadn't been for that crazy husband of yours, I would have been history. You took a big risk of losing Michael when you let him leave, and I deeply appreciate your concern for me."

Becky smiled as a tear of joy emerged from her watery eyes running down her cheek. "I'm just glad you're back," she forced out as a tear trickled off her chin. She turned her attention back to her husband who was in the process of greeting his son.

Bill knelt down face-to-face with Michelle. "I've got some bad news for you, Michelle. I'm afraid I lost your Bible before your dad arrived to rescue me."

"That's okay as long as you're all right," she whispered. Bill grinned as he patted Michelle on her curly golden crown.

"You're a good kid, Michelle, and don't let anyone stop you from going to Sunday School and believing what you know is right. Because of your Bible, I now know what is right too. I'll buy you any Bible you want as soon as we get back home." Bill gave her a big hug.

Suddenly the booming voice of the colonel echoed through the corridor, "Hansen, your time is up! Let's go!"

Michael looked at Becky, Michelle, and Marty. "I won't go anywhere without my family. You can ask us all the questions you want right here or take all of us back to the interrogation room. We have nothing to hide from them."

Colonel Stone doubled his fists, enraged with anger. "If this weren't so blasted important, I would have had you incarcerated hours ago and thrown away the key!" he screamed pushing everyone back in the two room chamber.

"Thank you," Michael said graciously, heaping coals of fire on the colonel's head. Becky took the kids in the bedroom while the three men sat down with Mr. Blackman again guarding the door.

"Now, from the beginning, where did you get the plans for your craft?" Stone demanded.

Bill glanced over at Michael. He returned the look with a slow nod of approval. "I drew up the plans myself with no other input from any other individuals or sources involved."

"Who else knows about this contraption and its capabilities besides your immediate family and Senator Duncan?" Stone asked jotting down the information in his notebook.

Michael shook his head no as Bill replied, "No one." Then he thought for a moment and added, "Unless you want to count the King of Egypt in 2351 B.C.! Unfortunately I was forced to give him a little flight around his kingdom."

"So that's where they got the idea for those hieroglyphic paintings of men flying in little space crafts!" Michael chuckled.

Bill turned to him trying to explain, "I had no choice!"

"Sure," Michael rebutted. "I bet you were just showing off."

"Gentlemen," the colonel interrupted, "May we continue? As I understand it, no one else in this era knows of your invention. And as I understand my orders from the Pentagon, we must keep it that way."

Bill and Michael questionably looked at each other as the colonel continued. "Apparently you were cautious or lucky enough, Mr. Abrams, on your venturesome trip back in time, not to do anything to have inadvertently changed the course of history. Your next trip back, you may not be as fortunate. Because of a confrontation you have with someone in the past may cause someone from this era to cease to exist. That confrontation could even cause other people or nations to be in power today. I assume you can understand our concerns. We were fortunate enough to discover the senator's financial information you provided for him, Mr. Hansen. We immediately relieved him of it before any action was taken. Do you realize what information like that could do to our financial markets? One person could accumulate the wealth of the world in a matter of days!"

A sickening feeling subdued Bill as he listened to the colonel. He could foresee his plans of returning to the past and regaining unmistakable proof of the creation fading away into government bureaucracy.

"Can you imagine all the things a person would be tempted to do if they had this capability? People would be going back to try and save loved ones from serious accidents. Athletes would attempt to change the outcome of sporting activities. Other people would jump ahead wanting to know what the future held for them. All financial markets would be shot to pieces by those trying to make a quick buck." Stone reasoned.

By now the colonel had arose and began pacing the floor while Bill and Michael looked on. "For these reasons, the United States Government is forced to hold your invention until a time we deem the people can control the use of it. We will significantly compensate you for the time and effort you have contributed to this invention, even though the government will not be using it. We simply cannot afford to take the chance of this information falling into the wrong hands. Unfortunately gentlemen, you will not be able to speak of your findings or your journeys to anyone. Nor will you be allowed to reconstruct in any way, shape or form, a device similar to your previous vessels. Additionally, you or any of your family will not be permitted to leave the United States. Uncle Sam has big ears and big eyes, and if either of you attempt to do anything I have mentioned, we will construe that as meaning both of you.

"To spell this out more precisely, let's assume Mr. Abrams decides to try something foolish, like fleeing from the country. We, in turn, will search out Mr. Hansen and his lovely family and take appropriate action. Do you get my drift, Mr. Abrams?" Colonel Stone leaned over the table glaring directly at Bill.

Bill reluctantly nodded his head yes while Michael let out a deep sigh of disapproval. "I assume we don't get to keep anything from the Light Assimilator?" Bill questionably stated.

"That is correct," Stone answered. "We have already relieved you of all your spare supplies, building plans, computer files and notes from your home. As stated before, our proposed settlement should cover everything adequately."

"I don't want your money!" Bill dramatically argued rising up from his chair. "I want my freedom!"

"Freedom to do what, Mr. Abrams?" the colonel questioned. "Go back and change the course of history affecting millions of people today? For the safety and freedom of this country, we cannot allow that. I hope you understand 'our position. We would love to use this idea for the space program, but we can't risk the consequences."

Bill contested, "Do you understand that I could bring you and the world absolute proof of how the world began and evolved? Our history books could be rewritten with real facts instead of just theories."

"And what would these facts be, Mr. Abrams?" asked the colonel snootily.

Bill hesitated for a moment. "It would be exactly as the Bible states. It is correct from the Garden of Eden on down to Noah's Ark and the Great Flood."

Holding out his right hand, Stone stopped Bill right there. "That gives me all the more reason not to let you go back. If we released your facts, supposedly proving the Almighty God created this world, we would be the laughing stock of the entire planet. Scientists would abandon the United States as a place to receive funds and conduct tests concerning evolution. With your conclusions, thousands of researchers would be eliminated from their current jobs. And no matter what proof you brought back, the majority of the American people would not believe it. Even though you just told me, and I know you were there, I still don't want to believe it and probably never will."

Bill turned to Michael. "Do you believe me, Michael?"

"I have to. I saw the Ark," Michael replied. "I can't help but know you're telling the truth."

"I don't want to hear anymore," Colonel Stone said as he headed for the door. "You folks are free to leave when you're ready." Mr. Blackman opened the door, and the two men left the room.

"I can't understand why God in all his wisdom wouldn't have allowed me to prove to millions of people there is no doubt about His existence and the validity of the Bible?" Bill asked not expecting an answer.

After a moment of silence, Michael did give this response. "Did you ever consider that God didn't want people to be able to prove

He exists? Maybe He only wants followers who can believe in Him without physical proof before their eyes or in their hands." Bill raised his eyebrows and gave Michael a look like maybe he was right.

At that moment, Becky stuck her head out the door of the adjacent room. "We're all packed and ready to go whenever you are."

"The sooner we get out of here, the better," Michael resounded. "AMEN!" piped in Bill. "What does Amen mean, anyway?"

"So be it," stated Michelle.

"Well, so be it," responded Bill energetically grabbing the few bags Becky and the kids had. "Let's get out of here," he added as the five of them walked out of the room.

Once outside of the federal building Becky asked, "What now?" as they headed down the front steps.

"Say Bill!" Michael exclaimed. "We've got an offer from the French archeologist Pierre Neesto. He wants us to head a dig he's orchestrating in New Mexico in a couple months. What do you say we go throw a little dirt?"

"I don't think so," Bill earnestly responded. "I've got a story to tell to this nation."

"Now wait a minute," contended Michael. "You heard what the colonel said. If either of us gets caught spreading information about your travels, all of us have to pay the consequences. I personally can handle that, but I have a family to be concerned about."

"Not that story," explained Bill. "I wholeheartedly believe what I saw on my journey and what is written in the Scriptures. The 30 days I spent patiently waiting for you, I read and studied the remainder of Michelle's Bible. I have the faith and conviction that the entire Bible and its teachings are correct. That will be my message. I can now convey to others how the Bible's account of creation fits perfectly with what science says. Dinosaurs once ruled the earth, a flood covered the earth, an Ice Age froze half of the planet, and numerous changes have occurred to this world. Science just needs to understand these changes occurred catastrophically and not gradually!"

"And someday, when the government allows me to use the Light Assimilator again, I will show this not-so-old world some things they would never believe. And maybe some things that are yet to come." Bill's voice faded as he opened Michelle's pocket Bible to the book of Revelation. "Until then I am going to spread the Word with all my heart, all my mind, and definitely all my soul.

I've seen the Light!"

THE END

BIBLIOGRAPHY

Farrell, Vance	The Evolution Cruncher	2001
God	The Bible, NIV	1400 B.C. – 100 A.D.
Henderson, Ken	Taming Dinosaurs	1976
Patten, Wesley Donald	The Biblical Flood and The Ice Epoch	1971
Ranney, Wayne	Carving Grand Canyon	2006
Wysong, R.L.	Creation-The Evolution Controversy	1997

CPSIA information can be obtained at www.ICGtesting.com
Printed in the USA
LVOW10s0611030615

440888LV00002B/4/P